This edition first published 2020 by Fahrenheit
Thirteen, an imprint of Fahrenheit Press.

ISBN: 978-1-912526-67-3

10 9 8 7 6 5 4 3 2 1

www.Fahrenheit-Press.com

F 4 E

Slow Bear

By

Anthony Neil Smith

Fahrenheit Thirteen

An Imprint of Fahrenheit Press

Also by Anthony Neil Smith and available from Fahrenheit Thirteen
- *The Butcher's Prayer*
- *Trash Pandas*

This book is dedicated to Lucille, my three-legged cat.

*Also, a hat tip to Jim Harrison and Jim Crumley,
who could write this shit a lot better than I ever will.*

CHAPTER 1

Micah "Slow Bear" Cross slouched at the casino bar, as usual, late that morning with half a beer in front of him when this guy named Jim sidled up on the next stool. Jim nodded at the Bartender Lady, slid two chips worth forty bucks over to Slow Bear and said, "I bet my wife is cheating on me. Can you find out if she is?"

Slow Bear, with his right hand, his only hand anymore, slid the chips back. "Hell, Jim, I know your wife is cheating on you. Everybody knows that."

Jim cringed. Stared at the bar.

"And it's with that light-skinned pit manager. Vlad, I think his name is."

"That fucking slut. That whore."

"And another thing. You already knew that. All you wanted was someone to justify it. That new gun you bought off Paul? I'm telling you, killing the man is not gonna help. You'll go to jail, and she'll fuck other guys anyway." Slow Bear reached across for one of the chips, pulled it back his way. "That one I'll charge you for."

Jim took the other chip and left without a thank you or a fuck you or anything. That was the way people treated Slow Bear. Never a thank you, never a fuck you, never much of anything besides some free chips and a problem to solve. He took another pull of his beer. Warm as morning piss. He'd been pulling at it for three hours. People thought he was a burned-out drunk but that wasn't true. Most of the time he was burned-out sober.

Later, he bet the chip on a hand of blackjack and kept hitting until he busted, on purpose. He didn't want Jim's money. He didn't like Jim. He kind of liked Vlad. Shame Jim was going to kill the bastard. Well, he could try. Slow Bear called Vlad and told him what was up.

Slow Bear used to be a rez cop. He wasn't good at it, not really, but he was good at being bad at it. The one time he tried to be good at it, he got his whole fucking left arm shot off by an ex-soldier over something that happened in a war Slow Bear didn't know much about. That was a year ago.

Now he collected disability and, weirdly, a settlement from the gun company that built the shotgun, some genius move by his not-that-cheap lawyer. Plus his payout for being an Indian, that wasn't a drop in the spittoon. It gave him enough of an income to sit around at the casino during the day, giving people like Jim and Vlad "advice" on their problems in exchange for some chips. At night he went back to his trailer and sat outside staring at the sky or inside at the TV—baseball games or Cinemax soft-porn—or, very seldom, he would drive, man, drive, as far as he could in circles until he was too tired, then pull off on the shoulder and fall asleep, usually awakened by a cop before dawn who would sometimes buy him a coffee at the nearest Arby's and trade cop stories. Slow Bear had run out of cop stories and started making them up. No one cared.

That night, he was sitting on the sundeck of his vintage red-and-chrome Richardson Bi-Level trailer—what a find, man, what a find—in a molded-plastic Adirondack chair. All the lights out, watching those stars and, if he turned his head right, nebulas. His eyes were getting more sensitive. There were more new, distant galaxies and clusters and shit every time he sky-watched. He had learned to distinguish the noises—crickets, coyotes, moose, far-up there jumbo jets, not-so-distant trains carrying oil from the boom. Not much traffic where he'd decided to settle on the rez, some badlands, sparsely peopled, one tree in his yard. So he heard the car a long time before he saw the headlights. Once he saw the lights, he stood. There was no other reason for anyone to be out here except to see him, and that meant something bad.

He walked back down the steps into the trailer, grabbed his

.357, and stepped out onto the ground to wait, slipping behind his one tree, out of the way of the lights that would soon blind him reflecting off the trailer. No surprises. He never wanted to be surprised again. Slipped his gun into his jeans so he could wipe sweat off his palm. Goddamned one hand.

Here they came.

Gun out again.

The car was a little Chevy, a Cruze. The driver was fast. He skidded to a stop next to Slow Bear's pick-up truck and a dust cloud overtook them both. Slow Bear knew the car. He put his gun back into his jeans.

Vlad jumped out of the car and ran for the trailer door.

"Over here."

Nearly gave Vlad a heart attack, looked like. A squeal, an honest to God squeal. He changed course towards Slow Bear. "Micah, I need help, man, I need—" He got close enough to see the big revolver in Slow Bear's pants and stopped cold and held up his hands.

"Shit, Vlad. I'm not going to kill you."

"Please, please, I'm cool. I'm real cool," but he said it like he wasn't. "I need help, man."

Needing help was bad. It was real bad. Slow Bear felt it in his bones. In his phantom limb. "What did you do?"

"I don't know what happened, it was just, it was fast, man."

Vlad kept clearing his throat and he had puffy cheeks. He'd been crying. Slow Bear didn't even need his cop instincts to paint the scene for him. This was an easy one. And it was all Slow Bear's fault.

Slow Bear said, "What did you do?"

"It was self-defense, man, I had to do it."

Slow Bear stared off over the Cruze, still running. He eventually nodded, sighed. "Give me a minute. Need to get a couple things."

They rode back to New Town in Vlad's Cruze instead of Slow Bear's old Nissan Hardbody that still got him around. Vlad talked the whole time in a warbly sing-song that Slow Bear nodded and Mm hm-ed to while thinking of other shit. He had the things he needed in a plastic shopping bag, the top scrunched tight in his fist and held between his legs. It was a dark night, new moon. Gas flares from oil rigs in the distance, like Mordor.

"I don't know what happened. It was fast. I don't know. He came at me, but then he turned around. I didn't mean to. I didn't mean to. I would never have hurt her. I loved her. Loved her so fucking much."

"Wait, what? Her?"

"I don't know what happened."

Slow Bear slammed the back of his head against the headrest. Fuck. Poor Greta. Jesus Christ. "What did you do?"

Vlad, chattering teeth. "I-I-I don't know what happened."

"I thought you were going to kill Jim."

"It was…she was…it was both of them."

Just kill me now.

"Where's the gun?"

"What? My gun?"

"Do you have it? I'm going to need it."

Vlad thumbed at the backseat, what little there was of it. Slow Bear looked. It was a mess of Styrofoam go cups and junk mail catalogs and dirty towels. He couldn't reach from here. He'd wait until they got to the house.

The town was busy enough this time of night. People out in clusters of cars outside of bars or, shit, the school, the library, the firehouse. Headlights on, sitting on hoods, paper bags full of cheap hard booze, plastic grocery bags full of six-packs. Slow Bear remembered some guy telling him it was "misery porn," the stuff whites expected to happen on the rez. That guy was a poet. Slow Bear didn't read poems. He would've agreed that it was just a stereotype if he hadn't been a tribal cop during the oil boom. Jesus, the rez was rolling in dough now, and that had made things worse. Fucking meth. He'd had his share when he was younger. Happy he got his shit together before he drowned in it. But there was also heroin. That one was still tempting. It would never completely loosen its hold. Now that Slow Bear was a civilian again, getting "money for nothing," he could hear it singing to him, a sweeter song than the fucking pain pills that had stopped working.

Anyway, yeah, midnight might as well be noon to oil workers, pushers, users and drunks. Vlad had stopped his bawling and his constant "I don't know what happened" once he got closer to the house. Slow Bear told him to drive past once and then park out on the main drag across the street from one of the few bars in town, which also called itself a casino, the slots jammed into a space the size of a couple of janitor's closets.

They walked back to Jim and Greta's house once Slow Bear had gotten the gun out of the backseat—a .22 pistol, like he'd expected—and put it into his bag. He used an old taco wrapper to pick it up. The lights on the street were busted. Only house lights gave them an idea of who else was out, sitting on lawn chairs or wooden steps in dusty front yards, toking up, sipping whiskey that came in a plastic jug. So what if a few insomniac drunks saw them? Wasn't a soul on this rez ever going to give up Slow Bear's name. Not. One. Soul.

They turned up the driveway past Jim's Jeep Cherokee and Greta's Kia on the patch of dirt and grass that was supposed to be a front yard. The TV was loud enough to hear a couple feet from the door which, thankfully, was closed.

"Didn't lock it, did you?"

Vlad shook his head. "I don't even remember."

Slow Bear knelt on one knee and pulled a latex glove from his bag. Flexed it on most of the way, then used his teeth to pull it fingertip tight. He told Vlad, "Don't touch anything. Period."

Vlad nodded but Slow Bear knew he was going to touch shit. Tell people not to touch shit, they touch shit anyway. Slow Bear pushed himself up and opened the screen, then, with the lightest of touches, took hold of the knob and turned slowly. The door creaked open.

The TV was loud. The crab-fishing show was on. Lots of

bleeping. The tiny house, a cookie-cutter rez project like all the others on this street, built in, what, the seventies? Had the look of Civil War about them now, crumbling, peeling, sinking.

Inside, the scene was right there in front of them: living room, TV blaring, the back of a recliner, pitched high and forward like someone was slumping in it, a futon to the side against the wall, a coffee table knocked sideways, a free-standing lamp with a halogen bulb, casting shadows. A bare foot sticking past the recliner into Slow Bear's line of vision. The whole place smelled like microwaved food and the shit of the recently deceased.

The recliner had bullet holes in it.

"Fuck, Vlad. Self-defense? From behind?"

"I don't know what—"

"Are you an idiot? Are you a goddamned idiot?"

Slow Bear took several more steps so he could see what he had already guessed would be there. Jim, slumped over in the chair, three twenty-two bullets in his head, his shorts and briefs pulled down to his ankles. On the floor in front of him, Greta. More than three bullet holes in her and Slow Bear guessed maybe only one of the ones that killed Jim had gone through, maybe, his eye-socket or something and struck her, but not killed her, because she had been on her knees sucking Jim's cock. The rest of the bullets in her were scattered, like a man with a shaky hand. Like you'd see from a jealous husband catching his wife cheating. Never seen one where it was the lover more jealous.

"Jesus, Vlad."

"I swear! I swear! I don't know." The man wouldn't step inside any farther. That was okay. Slow Bear imagined there was Vlad DNA all over this place.

Slow Bear turned. "Close that door."

Vlad did. Then he stepped over to the corner and stood there like a little kid in trouble. Slow Bear pointed at him. "Good. Stay there."

Vlad nodded. Slow Bear strategized. He didn't want to

6

wander around and spread evidence of his being here—boot prints, hair, skin—any more than he had to. He tried to tune out the crab-fishing show on TV. And then Vlad started talking. "You told me he knew! You told me! I had to protect myself. I had to confront him. Greta wasn't happy with him, she wasn't, she told me she wasn't. I was going to tell him he should stay out of it, you know?"

Slow Bear sighed, yawned. Goddamn it. He started back towards the short hall past the living room—a small bathroom full of cheap make-up and expensive shampoo bottles, most of them empty, and a rust-stained tub. Two bedrooms, one for storage and one for sleeping and fucking.

Vlad was still going, "—Like, he got off on it? And she was into that? He says he knows about me and she starts telling him how we fucked, and he got hard, and she got hot, and and and—"

"That's not self-defense!"

"I don't know what happened!"

Vlad would keep saying that until he figured out something that he could believe. Or something Slow Bear would tell him that he would believe.

In the bedroom, Vlad still out there braying like Greta had betrayed him, it was easy to find what he was looking for. The box-spring and mattress for the queen-sized bed was on the floor, not a frame, and an upside-down Igloo cooler served as a bedside table for Jim—his watch, his video game controller, his candle-in-a-jar that smelled like apple pie, and the TV remote for a screen at the foot of the bed so big that it covered one of the sliding closet doors. Slow Bear first checked under the mattress, then the box spring. Nope. Then he tilted the cooler. There it was: a slightly-used-but-new-to-Jim Taurus made to look like a Glock, or a Springfield, yeah, more like a Springfield, all the arty lines and shit. It was a forty, for fuck's sake. Shame. No, he didn't think Jim really would've used it, but probably got it to make his dick feel bigger than it already was.

Vlad: "We were talking about having kids, man!"

Slow Bear grinned, glad Vlad couldn't see him. Vlad must not have known about the two she'd already had taken away, then the cancer scare, then the hysterectomy. All before she was thirty. And, hey, none of that made her a bad person. Slow Bear thought she was actually one of the better people he'd met as a cop. Some domestics, some drunk driving warnings, but all-in-all, she was off the dope and drank like a normal thirty-four-year-old who liked a good party after a week of night shifts at the casino reception desk.

Or, sometimes, after every shift.

Woman shouldn't be dead for giving her own husband a blowjob.

Slow Bear held the gun between his knees, pulled back the slide, chambered a round. Then took the gun and shoved it into his back waistband, felt like the damn thing was going to fall into his underwear. People must've worn tighter clothes on cop shows. But it held. He reached into the bag for the twenty-two, which held eight rounds. He had counted seven in Jim and Greta, one shared. One shot left. He hoped so.

He stepped out of the bedroom, walked down the hall, Vlad now quiet and staring at the TV, someone shouting about a rogue wave. Slow Bear shook his head, hand on his hip, holding the twenty-two.

"I don't know what to tell you. There's no way this is going to work as self-defense. Just no way."

"Aw, man, please."

"Seriously, you need to turn yourself in and plead, I don't know, crazy or something. I'm not sure I can really help you."

Vlad shook his head, rubbed his palms roughly against his scalp. "No, no, no."

"Well, I can only do so much."

Vlad looked up. "You're in it now. You're in it as deep as I am. That's what I'll tell them. This was all your idea." He pointed at Slow Bear. Actually pointed. "If you can't figure out a better plan, I'm going to tell them you were the brains behind it all."

What brains?

"Vlad, cool it–"

"Because I don't deserve this shit, man! I did what I had to do, just like you said."

"When the fuck did I ever say that?"

"In the bar, I swear, you did. You told me what to do, how to do it. I'm not going down alone. So you'd better help me here."

Slow Bear let out a deep sigh and took in the scene again. Jesus. What an idiot. And now threatening him, too. How'd this dumbass get through a full day on his own?

"You went in hot, didn't think it through."

"I don't know what—"

"Hey, hey, shut up for a minute. I'll show you what I mean." He took big slow steps across the room, careful for blood spatter, and then handed Vlad the twenty-two, handle first. "Take this."

Vlad came out of his corner, gingerly, and took the gun two-handed.

"Watch." Slow Bear made more careful steps until he was over in front of Jim, hoping the body would stay put. One in a million chance of the body staying upright like this. Perfect. He crouched, hand on his knee. "So you come in, and you stand back there behind him, sure. But you've got your gun in hand, but first you want him to know who was killing him, right?"

"I swear, I wasn't going to kill him."

For fuck's sake. "Fine, you were going to warn him. I don't care. But you called out his name, right?"

Vlad nodded.

"Meaning if he'd had this gun," Slow Bear reached behind for it, swung it out. "This would've happened."

He shot Vlad in the shoulder. Went clean through. Loud motherfucker, set Slow Bear's ears ringing, but he'd gotten used to close-up guns. His ears recalibrated fast. Vlad stumbled, yelped, lifted the twenty-two and squeezed off a wild shot, miles from Slow Bear or the bodies, and just kept clicking.

"And you get the son of a bitch with three shots, in the back of his head." He was thinking fast, missing all sorts of details, but he figured the cops would miss them, too, because it looked so fucking obvious. "But he's not quite done."

Two more shots. Slow Bear didn't want to make them look like someone who knew what he was doing. So one shot went wide, the other through Vlad's left lung. That was the killer. It might take a few minutes, but that one was it.

While Vlad strangled on his own blood, Slow Bear very carefully wiped the barrel against Jim's hand, transferring some residue, he hoped. But again, rez cops weren't going to go all out for this. He set the gun on Jim's lap, ready to put the dead man's hand on top of it, when he sensed something wasn't right. Jim started to slide. Fuck! Slow Bear dodged out of the way, and Jim fell right on top of his wife. She farted. Gas build-up. Still, pretty fucking freaky.

Slow Bear stood straight, closed his eyes and leaned his head back. Took in some deep breaths, trying to calm down. His muscles were knotted up, pulling tighter. Deep breaths through his nose.

In. Ouuuuut.

In. Ouuuuuuuuuut.

In? Cough. In. Ouuuuuuuuuuuuuuuuuut.

Opened his eyes and looked around. Vlad, still blinking. A hurt look, if Slow Bear had to describe it. Why, man? Why?

"You think you were going to take me down for your stupid bullshit? Live by the gun, die by the gun. Goddamned stupid, I tell you."

The light faded from Vlad's eyes. Good.

If he'd done this right, it would look exactly like it should've looked. Love triangle gone shitty. Guns and hot tempers. Ain't no one getting Slow Bear involved.

The neighbors weren't going to call the cops. Not yet. They had all heard both rounds of gunshots now but they all wanted some sleep, or at least to stay up without a goddamned light show on their street for the next however-many hours. So they would wait, call it in after coffee the next day.

But that also meant Slow Bear had to sit his ass here for a while, because even if the neighbors wouldn't tell the cops who they saw leaving the house after the shots, they'd sure as fuck tell each other, and word got around.

So Slow Bear retreated to the bedroom, slapped Call of Duty into the console, and shot motherfucking enemy soldiers—yeah, he spent a long time figuring out how to do it one-handed—until he was sure it was safe to leave. Out the back, through the back yards of several houses, and then in the clear. It was a long fucking walk back to his trailer. Oh well. He hadn't seen a sunrise in a while. And it wasn't like he had anything to do tomorrow anyway.

CHAPTER 2

Slow Bear didn't make it back to the bar at the casino til almost sundown the next day. He'd thought about finding a ride somewhere, or borrowing a bicycle, or anything, but he couldn't risk being seen wandering around out late. Didn't want handprints, fingerprints, smudges, nothing to do with this shit. He'd lifted some cash from their pockets, not cleaning them out because that would look like a robbery. No, he took enough that the cops wouldn't really miss it.

Anyway, back to the trailer by seven-ten the next morning, sweaty, filthy, tossed off his clothes and flopped face down onto his bed and almost immediately he was gone, dreaming of heroin as a red-haired lover like the girl from SNL. She had a mouth on her—she smiles and you see every last tooth she had—but she did it for him. In the dream she sucked on the business end of a syringe, filled with the good stuff, between showing off those perfect choppers.

Slow Bear couldn't lucid dream to make her do his bidding. He didn't want to wake up, either. It had been a while since he'd kicked horse and didn't want to board that train anymore, but if his brain was all like "Dream the junk feeling like it's this chick you dig spreading her pussy for you" then who was he to argue?

When he finally did wake in the late afternoon, like every fucking day he remembered he had one arm, not two like he dreamed, and ached all over so bad it made him want to puke.

He gagged up a puddle's worth of something alcoholic—sure as fuck wasn't beer and he remembered the vanilla vodka he drank straight from the bottle at Jim's place—and sat at the edge of the bed and stretched his jaws until some of the tightness faded away all over. Then a shower, some microwaved chicken fingers, and out for the evening.

He could've made a couple hundred already if he'd gotten there earlier, Bartender Lady said. Her name was Kylie and she had dropped out of college, but Slow Bear called her Lady because he was afraid for her but couldn't afford to get too involved. If she had her way, he'd be beating up her exes, her professors who failed her, her step-daddy, her ex-stepdaddy, and she'd still ask him to piss on her real daddy's grave. Then offer to pay him with a blowjob. Slow Bear had done the currency conversion in his head and found it wasn't worth it.

So he ordered the usual beer and waited, figured he'd end up on the losing end that night and was only doing this to keep the habit alive—this habit—in order to make sure he didn't fall back into the other one.

Heroin. A wide-mouthed, redheaded bitch who made him laugh.

He laughed.

Lady, her uniform shirt unbuttoned two buttons too much, told him, "Trevor was looking for you."

"Jesus."

"Twice."

Slow Bear took a swig. "Well, I guess I'll have to call this day a loss."

"You can duck behind the bar with me if you want, sit on the floor."

What the hell good would that…? "Thanks, Lady, but I don't think my back could take it."

She was cute. She dyed her hair red then blue and sometimes it was just dark brown, like now, and one side of her head was shaved. Her glasses were thick and she tried to distract from them with too many earrings and a nose ring. Chubby cheeks, baby fat all over. Why not, Slow Bear? Why not?

Because. She doesn't do it for me.

Also? Last time he fucked a chick? He couldn't keep his balance. Threw him off his game. After nine minutes of trying, the chick was done with it, offered to use her hand. He told her no and went home.

So, Trevor. Chief of the rez police. Used to work with Slow Bear, then was Slow Bear's supervisor, then Chief. Then ex-boss. And somehow they were related, long lost cousins, but then, who wasn't? Slow Bear drew his disability pay and stayed out of the way except, you know, shit like Jim and Vlad. Shit like cheaters and drug money rip-offs and "sold me a broken iPhone" and whatnot, stuff the cops couldn't enforce since neither side was right in the first place.

Slow Bear didn't need Trevor Cross on his ass that day. Slow Bear sometimes forgot he lived on a rez this small, only about four thousand residents still here out of about thirteen thousand tribe members altogether, because on days he had to drive far and wide, or nights he had to walk hell and gone back to his little patch of prairie, it felt like it stretched to the ends of the earth.

But size was relative. Trevor probably knew about the shooting as soon as Slow Bear had left Jim's house, even though he'd played his cards well. Slow Bear hoped Trevor appreciated his solution to the problem, saving everyone a night in jail. Three disbursements back into the pot. Everyone profited.

Slow Bear wished. He fucking wished.

Lady set a fully-dressed Bloody Mary in front of him—big ass pickle and garlic-stuffed olives and a hunk of queso on a sword, black pepper flakes all over.

"Hey, no. No."

She said, "Trust me. You'll need your strength."

"I don't even like them." He pushed it back. The black pepper made him sniff.

"Bet you've never tried one. I know for sure you've never tried mine. Got the habanero sauce." She leaned towards Slow Bear, elbows on the bar, good view of her tits.

Why him? Why?

Then her eyes flicked over his shoulder. She pushed up and away and went off to get some more beers for the oil workers and white tourists down the way. Slow Bear felt the shuffle and heat before the smell of the man wafted across the bar.

Trevor Cross. He took the stool next to Slow Bear and was uncomfortably close. They used to be friends, but they'd never sat this close as friends. Trevor looked like he was carved out of rock. No, not carved. Dynamite blasted, like the unfinished Crazy Horse one Dakota south of there.

Trevor cleared his throat. Laced his fingers on the bar, arms wide, encroaching on Slow Bear's space. Slow Bear picked up the giant mug of Bloody Mary and gave it a try. Aw, fuck, that was gross. He bit the end off the pickle before setting the concoction down.

"Micah."

"Trevor."

"You know where I was all morning?"

Slow Bear turned his head, but didn't want to look in the Chief's eyes. One good blink and he looked back at the Bloody Mary. Picked the cheese hunk off the tip of the sword. "I hear you've been hanging around the bar looking for me. Seems like a waste of your day."

"Only partially true." He whistled for the bartender. Shouted, "Coke Zero."

Next, an olive. Lady was right about Slow Bear needing his strength. Last night was all reflex. It was as fast as he could think. Some homespun justice, keeping his own mostly innocent self out of the picture. He needed some long-term lying skills in play.

Slow Bear shrugged. "I have no idea." He took another slug of Bloody Mary. Disgusting.

"What's up with you today? You're usually earlier than this."

"Took a 'me' day. My stomach hurt."

"Something you ate?" He thanked the girl for the Coke and turned on his stool, framing Slow Bear between his wide knees. Goddamn it. Slow Bear took a sip of beer. Bad after the Bloody shit.

"Maybe it's catching. Might want to sit back."

"I was over at Jim's earlier."

"Hey, how is he? I was over there a few days ago, playing

Xbox." DNA, check.

"You were talking to him yesterday. Did he pay you for something?"

"I ripped him off. I mean, what he wanted wasn't worth what he paid."

"Maybe you should've listened." His breath smelled like chewed gum. Slow Bear didn't know how someone with fresh-chewed gum mouth could stand to drink a Coke. "Because maybe you could've given him some better advice. Maybe the man would still be alive."

Slow Bear finally turned, eyebrows up. "Suicide?"

Trevor rolled his eyes. He took off his cap and rubbed his palm over his hair, slicked back so it looked wet, but Slow Bear knew it was rock hard gel. Fitted the cap back low, right above his eyebrows. "Something like that, except murder."

Slow Bear deflated, as if it had hit him so hard. He knew how to act. He knew that Trevor saw through it, but Slow Bear still felt...something...like, obligation, maybe. An obligation to lie his ass off.

Slow Bear said, "Well, shit."

"Him. Greta, too. But at least the killer didn't get away. You know Vlad, right? Looks like Jim tagged him before his own soul flew free."

Sighed. "Stories like that make me glad I retired."

"Bullshit."

A shrug. "You're right. I miss the smell of blood."

Trevor slid off the stool and wrapped an arm around Slow Bear's shoulders. Got his face in close. "The fuck did you do in there? Why didn't you leave Vlad alive for us? One call. I would've believed you."

A swig of beer. Still didn't taste good. It never tasted good anymore. Slow Bear shook his head harder. "No idea, Trev."

Trevor gripped hard. Too close now. "It wasn't your call to make."

Slow Bear thought Fuck it. "I saved you a trial. I saved you having to jail that piece of shit. I saved you the messy shit. What it looks like now is the way it should've looked. Clean.

16

Justice."

"Your justice is dollar store justice, you goddamn—"

"Are you going to arrest me? Fine. You know my lawyer. Look what he did last time. It ain't possible, what you're saying, a one-armed man to have done—"

"For fuck's sake, it still wasn't your call."

Slow Bear thought about it for a second. Then another sip of beer. "Mm hm?"

Trevor pushed off and growled. Brushed his sport coat back and put his hands on his hips, the left just above his pistol. Circled. Twice. Staring at a line of automaton old folks pressing buttons on slots, immune to the clanging.

Slow Bear peeked over his shoulder. He knew Trevor probably had a witness saw him with Vlad. Trevor could figure things out because he was a smart cop. But what could he actually prove?

Getting his fucking shoulder blown clean off by that lunatic in a meth lab trailer had actually saved Slow Bear from corruption charges already. Gave him a graceful exit sort of thing. Colored over his bad choices with some last-minute heroics. Getting shot was always a surefire way to get called a hero.

But he had to face it, as he had on the walk home, over and over, it shouldn't have been his call, like Trevor said. Did he really think no one would figure it out? His flimsy triple-murder diorama?

Because Vlad was trying to wrap battleship chains around his neck, let them go down together forever?

You know why? You really know why? Because Vlad fucking de-served it. People should get what they deserve. Slow Bear laughed to himself. Really? If he believed that...Slow Bear mimed a finger gun to his temple. Bang.

Lady saw it. She rolled her eyes. He winked at her.

Trevor was back. Slid onto the stool again. "The Hat told me to say hi for him."

"The Hat! Really?"

"Oh, yes. He's very concerned about you."

This tickled Slow Bear to no end. The Hat was THE CHIEF (well, "Chairman," anyway) of the rez. The whole damned bunch of them. They called him The Hat because that's what he wore in public, whenever there was an audience of some sort, or a TV camera, or photographers. A giant custom-made beaver fur cowboy hat. Clean as the day it was delivered, damn near ten years along now. But that wasn't saying The Hat was just a "hat," without any bonafides. When he was a young man, well before his current age of teetering on sixty, his hats were all dirty and torn and that was when he could afford a hat at all. So now that the man ran the tribe and had become an oil tycoon while doing so, more power to him and his humongous, clean hat.

"How is The Hat these days?"

"He's good, real good. I was talking to him this morning, while avoiding bloodstains all over Jim's carpet, you know, and your name so happened to come up."

"Helluva a guy, that Hat." Slow Bear had met him a handful of times, the first couple being brush-offs, the next two, "What the fuck were you thinking, Officer?" and then the last, in the hospital, shaking Slow Bear's remaining hand, giving him a key to the rez, or not, maybe he dreamed that part. But whispering, "Don't play the victim. You got really fucking lucky."

"Just so happens, huh?"

"Anyway...you know about the Exile. Santana. You know his story."

Slow Bear did. He did indeed. Every Indian on the rez knew his story because Santana was the only man besides The Hat who would have ever had a prayer of being Chairman...until The Hat made damned sure to squash that spark out like a bug.

Santana Hunts Along. His mom a true hippie, named him after goddamned Carlos Santana. A lot to live up to. And man, Santana sure as hell tried.

What brought him down was, honestly, the same thing that got The Hat where he is. Santana tried to go around The Hat to get a piece of oil action, a better deal for the people than what The Hat was giving them—jobs, sure, but where was the money? Like with the casino, where was the money?

"Invested," The Hat said. "Invested. For all of you." And he showed lots of spreadsheets and paperwork to back that up.

Santana should have—should have—called utter bullshit on him, but instead tried to politician his way around it. Sneaky. Problem with sneaky is that the other reps on the board were getting some of that "investment" straight into their pockets (as was Santana, let's be honest), and before long there was another stack of paper and spreadsheets showing that it was Santana Hunts Along dealing dirty, not The Hat.

Slow Bear knew all this because he was still a cop then and had the inside gossip. The outside gossip wasn't far off the mark, either. Jailing Santana would mean the end of The Hat's support in the tribe. He needed to be top Indian to keep the oil contracts the way he wanted them. So he gave Santana a way out—exile. Leave the rez and cut his ties, business and political. Make it sound like he was doing it of his own accord.

And wouldn't you know it, Santana did just that. Left town. Left the rez. Relocated to Williston and got hired on by another oil company, miraculously, and was well-off by anyone's standards, a tycoon by rez standards.

That was the story. That was what Trevor was talking about.

Slow Bear shrugged. "What about him?"

"The Hat thinks Santana never really broke off his ties over here. Just hid them. The Hat is convinced he's still working with the company, still getting checks, and that the company is pulling one over on us. That violates the deal."

"Not like it was a legal deal."

"Still. The deal was to avoid legalities and avoid a big fight. A big split. And you fucking know it, too."

"What do I know?"

"Jesus. Are you taking this seriously?"

"I'm about to call the day a total loss and head back home.

Seriously, man. I take that seriously." Slow Bear stood up. "I don't know why you're telling me shit about The Hat and The Exile, like some fucked up fairy tale. Is it a warning? You kicking me out?"

Slow Bear slapped the bar a couple of times to get Bartender Lady's attention. She looked over and he said, "No cash today. Get you tomorrow?"

She huffed, like this was a regular thing. The drinks were free while he gambled, of course, but for him that usually meant a dollar's worth of poker hands, stretched over a couple of hours. Today, he owed her three bucks.

Trevor said something. Slow Bear wasn't paying close enough attention, plus all the clanging. But when he thought on it a second, him asking You kicking me out? and Trevor, did he really say it? Yeah, Trevor answering, Sort of.

Slow Bear cleared his throat and nearly choked on the last drops of warm beer. "Excuse me?"

"It wasn't my idea. My idea was to take you in and let your ass rot in jail. Let some of the inmates you wronged discuss their grievances with you."

"Is that right?"

"Sit down."

Slow Bear did. Then he got some phantom limb pain on his missing elbow and reached to squeeze it. Goddamn, looked like an idiot. Lost his concentration. "You know I'm right. You know Vlad did it and instead of helping him cover it up, I delivered some righteousness."

"We're past that. Listen."

"So what do you want? Money? A bribe? Why would you want money from me? You know I'm barely scraping. I've kept a low profile."

"Shut up. Shut up and listen. Just shut up."

"Jesus."

"The Hat would like you to get in with Santana's operation and find some proof. And, this is important, if there isn't any, make sure that there is."

"What? Are you fucking me?"

"If it doesn't come easy, let me know. I'll give you something too good to be true."

Slow Bear shook his head. "You're assuming a lot."

"Possibly. There are ways around that."

"I mean, it's not like a one-armed Indian can go undercover just like that." He paused. "You hear that? It was the non-snap of my non-fingers."

"I said we'll deal with it."

"How? Magic?"

Trevor shook his head. "As far as Santana needs to know, you'll be banished just like him."

Slow Bear smiled. Yeah, a downright honest smile for once. "Why the fuck would he believe something like that?"

"Because that's the truth."

Trevor grabbed Slow Bear's beer bottle and slammed it onto Slow Beer's forehead once, twice, three times before it shattered, and Slow Bear felt pulverized, then there was ringing in his ears and blood leaking into his eyes. He fell off the stool onto his bad shoulder and got his feet tangled in the stool legs, twisted his ankle and the damned stool fell on top of him.

He shoved it out of the way. He'd bruised himself all over and was still blinking blood and glass away. That's when Trevor kicked him in the gut.

Noise, like a seal barking, that he realized was Lady shouting at Trevor to stop. But, fuck, when a man kicks you in the guts, you seize up and feel like you have to take a shit, so you clench back there, and that makes you hurt all over.

Then there was Trevor's shadow, the Chief leaning over Slow Bear, hands on his knees. "I'm sorry, Micah, but we have to make this look real. I'm going to kick your ass all over this casino, and then cuff you and drag you out to the truck. From there, we'll improvise."

Slow Bear barely heard, but got the gist. He rolled onto his stomach, pushed his chest half-off the ground and tried to drag himself away. That second hand would've been really helpful in this situation, but he had to work with what he had.

21

Trevor grabbed him by the collar, goddamn trying to choke him now, and pulled him upright. Still on his knees. The lawman took Slow Bear by the jaw and squeezed. "And then I'm going to impound that fucking trailer of yours, and your truck, too, and freeze your bankcard, credit cards, do you even have any credit cards?"

Slow Bear wanted to tell him he had a gas card, left over from his cop days. He had no idea who paid it, if anyone. But because he was shaking all over and the aches were rolling through his guts like a bad boat wake, he managed to say, "Fuck your mother, asshole."

Trevor backhanded his face. Slow Bear fell over again. If this was a movie, he would laugh and spit blood on Trevor's shoes or something, but this was real life and Slow Bear said, "I'm sorry I'm sorry I'm sorry ohgodohshitohgod, please!"

He finally opened his eyes all the way and saw a blurry crowd of people watching, and one of the security guards–not coming to help, but holding back the spectators–and now Lady trying to get to Slow Bear but getting shoved back by Trevor first, and then a second security guard, a fat pimply fucker grabbing her around the waist and getting a little too personal.

Trevor lifted his boot and raked it across Slow Bear's ear. Slow Bear felt the rough-bitten leather, gravel, dried gum, hobnails. He rolled away quickly, too dizzy, and pushed up again before Trevor gave him another kick square in his back, sent him sprawling. He was done.

The cop finally settled on his knees beside Slow Bear and cuffed his one wrist, then, like he'd forgot about the lack of another arm, let out a deep breath and said, "Well, fuck."

CHAPTER 3

Trevor drove him to the hospital. He wasn't a total monster. They all had their parts to play, he'd shouted into the backseat of his extended-cab truck on the way over while Slow Bear groaned, in a fetal position, feeling every pothole more than he ever had before.

"I wouldn't say it if I had a dash cam recording this shit, but I'm glad you killed the motherfucker. He'd been causing drama for weeks. Already pulled him in drunk and sad like six times. You ask me, I think Jim was into it. All part of a game they played, her fucking another man. Coming to you, that was just him playing the jealous boyfriend. She was watching when he did that."

"Aw, fuck." Clenching his gut again.

"I know, right? I wouldn't blame you. But this is what The Hat thought was best. Look at it like an opportunity."

"Goddamn!" Seething.

"No, man, no. Listen. You pull this off, you're in. I'm serious. Fuck that disability pay. You'll get some prime real estate and a nicer payout. And not one word about this bullshit with Vlad ever again."

It sounded wonderful. It sounded terrible. It sounded like noise being filtered through all sorts of pain.

He forgot several of the hours after that. Flat out forgot them, as if they'd never happened, a miracle of modern medicine, whatever painkiller they had pumped into him. Couldn't tell you nothing that was said to him nor done to him that whole time. Stitches? Staples? Wrapped his ribs?

He woke up not in a hospital, but with an aching neck in the passenger seat of a small car, shins so hard against the dash it was giving him splints. And for fuck's sake they were moving. Felt like the open sea, but it was instead the prairie at sundown.

Crick in his neck, shins on fire, ribs screaming, and some infernal itching where they'd stitched his ear, his forehead, and the back of his scalp. He shimmied himself up, drawing out a groan as he did. A look to his left, there was the Bartender Lady, out of her work uniform now, spilling out of a thin-strappy tank-top and fake-faded jeans and flip-flops.

She dropped her chin and glared at him over the top of her glasses. "Blurry does wonders for you right now."

He reached up for the sun visor, pulled it down and flipped the mirror. She was right. Clear as he could tell, there was a goddamn walking dead looking back at him.

"No wonder it hurts."

"I can't even imagine."

He sat quietly for a long time, watching the prairie pass them by, long shadows in the deep orange light, and let out a loud breath. "Where are we going?"

He already knew she was going to say Williston.

"Williston."

"Yeah, let's not. How about we turn around and go back home?"

Lady shook her head. "He said you've been banished. I'm not supposed to show up again until after I've dropped you off."

"How'd you get roped into this?"

A shrug. "I volunteered."

He barked. Supposed to be a laugh. "Why?"

She gave him one of those faces the youngsters pull off so well, absolute disdain. "I happen to kind of like you, you know."

"No, really."

"It was either this or you went in the back of a squad car."

His cheeks were growing hot. Her bare arms, her boobs right there, seriously, this shirt showing off most of her chest. Chubby, cute, and he'd been flirting with her a solid year now, hadn't he?

"If you want me, let's do this." He said. "Pull over, we can do it right now, then go home."

She rolled her eyes. "Jesus. I like it a little rough, but not sad. I can wait."

Nothing wrong with that. Before, it would've been like taking advantage of her. But now that she'd thrown herself in head first, maybe he could.

His shoulders dipped thinking about it. No, still, something felt off. She deserved better than him. Much better.

He looked around the car, a shitty little nondescript import. At his feet, receipts for drive-through coffee and burgers. In the back, a stack of old towels, textbooks abandoned when she quit school, and some spare bottles of motor oil on top of a box he assumed was her "cold weather kit," probably like most people's, full of expired food, some old flares, other things that might keep a person alive one more hour than they would have lived otherwise.

"This your car?"

"Yeah. All mine. Five-hundred bucks. I'm not even sure what it is. As long as it works."

"Don't we have…did you bring…where's your stuff? Where's my stuff?"

"Didn't have time, and I was told to steer clear of your place. The Chief gave me an escort to the border of the rez, too. So now you've got to tell me. What did you do?"

He slumped. Screwed, he was. Screwed, so screwed, was he. "Littering."

Her turn to laugh.

Then he said, "I forgot to clean up my mess."

"Bullshit."

"Don't worry about it. It's politics." God forbid she ever find out about Vlad. After all, they'd worked together, sort of. Maybe they'd talked when he got bored. Maybe they'd bumped into each other clocking in or out. Maybe they'd gone to middle school together. Maybe not but still, God forbid.

The car smelled like too-sweet shampoo and pretzels. There was warmish air flowing from the vents, all the windows cracked a little. He realized he was a sopping mess—his jeans filthy, his cowboy shirt sticking to his skin, and Lady's own skin was slick like a mirror.

"Hot in here."

"I didn't want to wake you." But now she rolled down the window and flopped her arm out, fingers spread wide in the wind. The roar made talking impossible so Slow Bear rolled his own down and reclined the seat. He didn't want to go to Williston. Again. He'd been there often enough as a cop—as a dirty cop—collecting cash from roughnecks and their bosses for a variety of reasons—look the other way, look for the wrong things, look at another guy instead. Or letting one guy skip jail for a price because the oilmen were short-handed and it was easier to pay Slow Bear than train in a new guy. And then there was the shit that led him to that trailer park, that half-assed meth lab, that lunatic with the shotgun.

He squeezed his eyes and shook his head. Not going to remember, but telling himself not to remember made him remember more, and he squeezed harder and shook harder. "Fuck."

"You okay?"

He sucked in a deep breath. Held it. Let it out. "You got, like, pain pills? Or weed?"

She pointed at the glove compartment. "Your pills are in there. I ain't got weed. I don't have the money for weed. Jesus."

"So what gets you there?"

She grinned. "Straight up beer, baby. Three of those, and I'm open for business."

A few pills did the trick and he napped a little while, waking up to nightfall in Williston, the most popular shitty town in North Dakota, one would guess. Roads filled on both sides with parked cars. More like temporary homes. Some of these cars had come a thousand miles or more to get here, and they would never leave, at least not in the condition they arrived. The cars that still worked and weren't filled with broke, depressed men looking for work were bumper to bumper, horns blaring, gas fumes making the air go wavy, all those brake lights.

Lady passed the bar Slow Bear used to frequent, where darker-hued people felt most welcome to drink, hook-up, score, rather than get stared at by white supremacist wannabes outnumbering them at the other bars in town. "El Norte Revolucion."

"What?"

He thumbed over his shoulder. "That bar. I liked that bar."

"You want to go?"

He shook his head, yawned. Felt himself drifting again. He told her, "No, let's…no."

She drove from hotel to hotel looking for a room, Slow Bear knowing she wouldn't find one. But then again, maybe she'd get lucky. Tits like those, maybe she had better sway.

But no, she got no play, no room, and he finally told her to try the Walmart parking lot. Not that he was fine with spending the night there, and not even sure they let people do it anymore like they did when the boom was new, but once he saw the makeshift village still spread across the asphalt, like a traveling circus without the elephants, he sighed. At least that was one problem out of the way. The next was making sure neither of them got jacked during the night.

Lady was a bit panicked. "I'm supposed to drop you off. That's it. Drop you off at a hotel, give you this hundred, and tell you not to come back until the time was right." She held up a much-folded hundred dollar bill between two fingers like a cigarette. He thought about telling her to keep it, but shit, he didn't know if Trevor could actually shut down his gas card like he'd threatened. So yeah, he took the hundred from her, put it in his pocket, gingerly.

He told her, "It used to be worse."

"What do you mean?"

"More cars out here, overflowing. More cars everywhere. Men everywhere. But the price of crude hit the floor, ran through the floorboards, and these rich motherfuckers are

27

cutting bait. No reason for the grunts to stay here anymore."

"Where will you stay?"

He reclined his seat as far as he could, settled his hand beneath his head, and said, "I was hoping…"

When it hit her, her jaw opened, eyes went wide. "No. Way. No. Way. I'm supposed to go back. I've got to work. I can't."

"Hell, it's late. Call in sick tomorrow, take your time getting back. Otherwise, I'll have to hide in the store until closing, and there's only a small chance I won't get caught."

She shook her head. "Just supposed to be a quick trip. That was all. No one ever said all night."

"Ever slept in your car before?"

She shook her head again.

"Goodnight, Lady."

For a long moment, he closed his eyes and was prepared to ignore her protests, but there were none. She turned off the motor and sat, both of them listening to it tik tik tik til cool, until finally he heard some rustling and opened one eye, looked over. She was, in that elegant way women could do it that men couldn't, taking off her jeans.

He said, "What the hell?"

"I'm not going to sweat like that all night."

She freed both legs. Slow Bear got a glimpse of fancy bright underwear between her rolls before the smell of her sweat hit him, further weakening his defenses. He lifted himself enough to peek out the windows, plenty of men out there standing around, some sitting on their car hoods, smoking. Others wandering, looking for a friend or two.

"Girl, you'd better hope nobody comes over and does whatever they've got to do to get to you."

She turned on her side, facing him. "As long as they don't try to get in, let them look."

"It's not safe."

"But I've got you protecting me, right?" A full-throated come-on if he'd ever heard one.

He sighed, reached into the back and pulled out a windbreaker that had seen better days. He draped it over her hip. "Your knight, ever shining."

Maybe they would get some sleep. Maybe not.

CHAPTER 4

The next morning they got a bag of biscuits, some coffee for Lady and orange juice for Slow Bear, at Hardee's. The girl sure could eat–she downed three biscuits to his two. She liked her coffee stupidly sweet, like, five packs of sugar, but no cream. Slow Bear had weened himself off coffee because of the price. Concentrated OJ was cheaper, and it mixed up well enough in tap water. What he wouldn't give for freshly squeezed, though.

They drove out to the address Trevor had given Slow Bear for Santana's main office. There was no guarantee he'd even be there. No guarantee he'd even be in town. Could be off making deals somewhere nice, like Alaska or Texas. But still, it was all he had to go on. Lady agreed to drive him since she had already called in to work, told them she had to take her uncle to Fargo for surgery.

Slow Bear was still groggy. He'd only napped periodically throughout the night. Of course Lady had pushed off the windbreaker when she'd been deepest asleep, and of course he awoke to some noise from three roughnecks peeking in on her. He got their attention, hiding the fact he had one arm, and reached for the glove compartment. That scattered them. He pulled the windbreaker over Lady again, sleep only coming in heated fits and starts until sunrise.

At the office, part of a complex of trailers that made up the company's HQ on the Bakken field, Lady parked and started to get out.

"Whoa, wait. This is the place, so you can go on back now. I'll send you a postcard."

"No one sends those anymore. Just text me."

"With what?"

"You ain't even got a phone? Come on, you've got a phone."

He held it up for her. "Battery's dead and I don't have a charger."

She pushed her door all the way open. "Right. You're in no shape to take on the oil industry alone. Come on. Need me to help you out?"

"Fuck no, I don't need—"

She smiled. He got the joke. He opened the door, kicked it wide, and pulled himself out of the car as if it was a space capsule.

The front office was exactly what front offices look like anywhere in Small Town, USA–right out of a catalog. Very new and very cheap. Desk, partitions, carpet, linoleum, file cabinets. Pre-fab smell. The woman at the front desk wore jeans and a shirt with tassels. Thin-haired blonde with cigarette fingers and gold-rimmed glasses. "Can I help you?"

In a chair across from her was a tough guy in khakis and a golf shirt, holstered gun on his belt. He looked up from his tablet–the reflection was bad, but did Slow Bear see naked lady bits on his screen? The man's eyebrows stood at attention over his reading glasses. Probably at Lady, whose strappy tank top might as well have been soaking wet or not even there.

Slow Bear cleared his throat. "Yeah, um, Santana. Mr. Santana Hunts Along. I mean, I want to see him."

The secretary flicked a look at the tough guy, then back. "Let me see, what's the name?"

"Cross. Micah."

A red thumbnail under her chin, staring at her flat-screen monitor. "I don't see it here. Could it be under something else?"

"Slow Bear. No, I mean, I don't have an appointment. But I'm…supposed to see him."

"Supposed to?"

"He wants to see me." Jesus, like he's ever done undercover work before. How did they do it? "Tell him I'm looking for a job."

The tough guy set his tablet down, laid his reading glasses on top of it, and stood. Held his hand out. "I think there must've been a misunderstanding."

They shook hands, the tough guy squeezing a bit too hard.

"I believe you skipped a few steps. Have you applied on our website?"

"Website?"

"Do you have experience in the field? On the rez?"

Slow Bear clocked Lady wandering the edge of the room, reading plaques on the wall, mostly oil-industry trade mags featuring Santana on the cover.

"Not that type of job. Not likely."

"Well I wasn't going to bring it up—" The tough guy held up his arm, the one Slow Bear didn't have. "You lose it out here?"

"Sort of. But, no, see, no." Sweaty palm. Rubbed it on his jeans. "What are you? Like, security? I've got references."

He knew it was going badly. He knew the tough guy was thinking tweaker. "Hey, let me ask you. You hear about a guy who got his ass tossed off the rez yesterday? Guy who used to be a cop?"

Headshake. "Not that I can say. Now, if you'd like—"

"Because don't I look like a guy who got his ass tossed off the rez yesterday? Ask Santana if he heard about me. One-armed cop from back home. Go on, ask."

The tough guy had crossed his arms during that spiel, turned and sighed. Him and the secretary did some "talking" with eyebrows and twisted lips.

By now Lady had drifted towards the chair where the tough guy had laid his tablet. She glanced down at the screen and said, "Shit!"

Definitely naked stuff.

"Hey—" The tough guy pointed a finger her way.

Slow Bear grabbed it, twisted down, almost the breaking point, but not quite. He still knew how. Fuck this guy.

He nodded to the secretary while the tough guy doubled

over. Lucky this was the tough guy's gun arm. He slapped his other towards his holster, but Slow Bear kept him off-balance, both of them stepping in a circle together, so he couldn't reach the gun.

"Mind calling Santana and tell him Slow Bear wants a meeting? It's urgent."

The secretary picked up the phone.

Three minutes later, Slow Bear pushed the tough guy–later learned his name was Manfred–through the door into Santana's office, which didn't look much like a big shot's office. Same shitty pre-fab flimsiness and smell, but with a full wall of windows looking out on flat, dry ground and some leftover building supplies. Buckets and discarded vinyl sheets and bags of quick-dry cement.

Santana, looking like the photos in the front office except not smiling, not even a little, reclined in his office chair, fingers laced over his chest. There were several other men in the office—two of them were dressed like Manfred and the other two were seated in the visitor's chairs in front of Santana's desk, both in suits—one with a tie, the other leaving too many buttons open on his shirt. Both in their fifties or sixties, both hoping they'd pass for forty.

"Promise me," Slow Bear said, putting a little more pressure on Manfred's arm, not knowing where the strength had come from. "If I let go, I'm still safe. Promise me, Santana."

Santana had the slow burn look of someone who got rattled way down deep inside, not out on the surface. Oh yes, retribution was going to suuuuuuck. This whole shitty carnival was a bad idea, and Slow Bear wanted to get out of it without anyone else beating him silly.

Santana nodded. "Sure, you're safe. Until I change my mind."

"Give me five minutes."

"Don't press your luck." Santana nodded at another security guy, who walked behind Slow Bear to the office door and shut it, the secretary and Lady getting a last look-see before it closed and clicked.

Well…he hadn't expected that.

Slow Bear let go of Manfred and danced back, boxer style. Light on his feet in case they wanted a fight. But Manfred stretched his arm, shook it, got some feeling back, and slowly, easily, took out his sidearm and pointed it at Slow Bear's head.

Slow Bear gagged, lurched forward and threw up a thin stream of hot acid and orange juice on the industrial gray carpet. He pinched his face in a bad way and tried to shove the rest of it out of his mouth with his tongue, apologizing between gags.

Finally, he lifted his trembling, nauseated head, and said, "My name's Slow Bear, and I used to be a cop, and I hear you could use a guy like me."

Santana stood, which made his visitors stand too, and said, "Jeeeeeeeesus. You're a wreck."

"It's been a bad week."

"Can we get him a towel? Anyone?" He hit a button on his phone. "Waterbug? Want to bring Mister Bear a towel, please? Do we have towels?"

The secretary said, "Right on it."

"Thanks, Waterbug." Click. "Her name's June, but she doesn't like Junebug, so I called her Waterbug one time after she brought me some water, and it stuck."

No one said a thing.

"Well, fuck all y'all, then. Just for that, I'm giving her a raise."

She knocked on the door, opened without waiting for an answer. She had a golf towel, one of those with a metal clip in the corner. She handed it to Slow Bear, who said, "Thanks kindly."

"Waterbug," Santana said. "They didn't like how you got your name, so you're getting another raise."

She rolled her eyes. "For fuck's sake."

"No, no, really. Add another three bucks an hour. Go fill out the paperwork."

Slow Bear turned to the open door. Lady was there with worried eyes, mouthing, You okay?

He shook his head. Waved her off. But he felt warm inside. That was real concern right there. The fact she liked him, especially enough to fuck him, made him feel damned toasty. But it also made him nervous whenever she was nearby. Like she'd regret it one day and make sure he got a raw deal to remember her by. One of those country songs, the guy cheats and the girl fucks up his truck? Shit, he needs his truck.

Santana shooed the suits out, walked out from around his desk. The office door clicked shut again and there was Manfred aiming a gun at Slow Bear, the other security man wishing he had someone to punch, and Santana buttoning his coat and shuffling his shoulders.

"Okay, Mister Bear. I'm guessing this didn't go the way you thought it would."

He wiped his mouth. "I wasn't thinking."

"You think I would hire you? That I should hire you?"

Slow Bear let out a deep breath, shook his head. "Not really. The Hat wanted me to come out here and spy on you because he thinks you're dirty. Maybe even dirter than The Hat himself."

Santana took a step back.

Slow Bear cringed. He felt another wave of puke coming on, but squashed it down. He hadn't planned to tell the truth until right before he did so. And he did so because, shit, he didn't want to do this anyway.

Santana unbuttoned his coat, put his hands on his hips. "You fucking with me?"

"My cousin, the Chief of Police, beat me up in public so this would be convincing. Part of my backstory. I didn't get a say in it."

"What does The Hat think I'm doing wrong?"

"Aw, man, it's a long story." Slow Bear told him what The Hat thought was going on, and how The Hat pretty much hated Santana's ever-loving guts and was jealous because of how the man had still succeeded in spite of the exile. "It's a fishing trip. I'm the worm."

Santana laughed and looked at his security guys like, Can you believe this? He stepped back around his desk and sat down in his high-backed chair, reclined again. He motioned towards one of the visitor chairs. Manfred finally holstered his gun and stepped out of the way. Slow Bear took a seat.

"In fact I have heard about you, of course I have. Got your arm shot off by some crazy Bosnian or Serbian? I get those confused."

A shrug. "Wrong place, wrong time."

"You used to make bank all over Williston, didn't you? Bought and paid for."

"Rented. I still had a personal life."

"Funny man. No, the way I see it is that you getting your arm blown to bits was a good thing. Saved you from having to pay society back."

Slow Bear nodded, finding it hard to look Santana in the eye. This man was the devil, just like The Hat believed. Slow Bear could feel it. Could smell it. Deviled eggs. "At the time, I wasn't thinking that. The first thing was the pain, you know. A shotgun blast is a motherfucker. And it didn't stop hurting for a long time. It still hurts sometimes. I still see my arm the way it looked the moment after, all wet and ripped to ribbons, bone shards, sort of a deep-fried feeling about it."

Santana grinned. "You know what I mean."

"Do I?"

"I like you."

"Do you?"

The businessman kept on as if he hadn't heard, spinning his chair to the side and slapping his palm on the desk to a rhythm of a song only he knew. "So how about, let's say, you be a double-agent? I feed you what to tell The Hat, and that helps him keep his pecker hard. When he's finally ready to blow, well, he learns I was faking the whole time. That might be fun."

Slow Bear slumped. "For you. I'm not supposed to set foot on the rez again until I've got you by the balls."

"There's only one good reason to stay on the rez, and that's if you run the place." He laughed. "Wait, wait, tell them I'm sex trafficking. Can you imagine? Just to see, I tell you, to see the look on The Hat's face."

Busted a gut, he did.

Slow Bear was too tired and sick to join in. His eyes kept closing and he tried to grin while Santana and Manfred tossed back things they could tell The Hat:

Shipping in illegals from Mexico.

Tax-evasion.

Polygamy.

Slow Bear woke himself to say, "Enough." And his hearing went ultra-sensitive the way it does when you wake up from a nap. The men's breathing and giggling, too loud. He worked his jaw a few times. "I appreciate the offer, but I'm not up for it."

"Seriously? It's free money to make some calls."

"Mm hm. But uhn-uh."

"Then why even come? You could've kept going." Santana's face, a miracle of good genes, this old son-of-a-bitch looking fresh and strong. It really was evil. "Why bother with showing off your strength, showing off your, your, I don't know. Moxie? People say moxie anymore? Showing off that girl of yours, for sure. A real rumpshaker you've got there. Girl's mighty healthy."

"Formidable," Manfred said.

Slow Bear sat up, ready to stand and go, but he was still feeling lowly. Pushed to the edge of his chair. "That girl is a fine girl, and she is my friend. I intend to take her home and deal with The Hat in person. He can only beat me purple so much before there's nothing left to bruise."

"Don't get me wrong," Santana, his fingers splayed, Stop...in the name of love. "I mean nothing intentionally hurtful. While I'm an admirer, I'm also objective. And your friend, my son, is a woman of particular heaviness."

Slow Bear stood. "Fuck you. Fuck your objectivity. Fuck your job. Fuck whatever it is you did to us when you fucked us over on the rez. Fuck it all, and then some."

Santana's smile crawled high on both sides like a living thing and became another laugh. A hack of a laugh. "Goddamn, I like him." He hit a button on his phone. "Waterbug, get three hundred out of petty cash. No, make it five. Five hundred out of petty cash for Mr. Bear here."

Slow Bear waved it off.

"No, I'm serious. You have entertained the dickens out of me today. You earned it. Go buy yourself some breakfast."

Slow Bear turned and left the office while the two men kept at it—Manfred saying, "I let him win"—then he was in the outer office, where the men in suits were drinking water from paper cones and Waterbug was standing next to Lady, counting out twenties into her hand. Then they hugged like best friends and Waterbug said, "Keep him out of trouble, darling."

Back outside, it was hot as balls again. The wind was up, you could watch it coming from far away and feel the heat of it suck the moisture from your mouth and lungs, replacing it with dust.

It was oddly quiet, too. Echoes of oil pumps and trucks, but not much else.

"What now?" Lady asked.

Like the man had said. "Breakfast."

CHAPTER 5

What he meant was coffee, mostly. Lady ate pancakes with fruit and whipped cream, even though they'd both had Hardee's earlier. This was a step up, a booth at a local café: Grandma's Sunny Day. Now that they had money, Slow Bear didn't think it was necessary to avoid coffee anymore, but he still got orange juice on the side. It was a thing now. Caffeine, sugar, bam bam bam! The queasiness had gone once he started pouring that mixture down his throat.

He felt good enough to order eggs. A la carte. Three scrambled eggs. Wasn't much better food in the world than scrambled eggs.

"Pretty stupid," Lady said with her mouth full. "I dream of jobs like that."

"He wasn't offering dental."

"Who cares? You could buy your own insurance with that kind of money. Can you imagine? It would be like, like, like writing for TV. You make it up. You tell the Hat about it once a week, and you're done. Cha-ching."

Cute. He grinned. "Let's go home. If I'm quiet, if I behave, maybe Trevor will leave me alone. I really want to be left alone."

"What did you do in the first place?"

"Let's not go there."

"Seriously, I've never seen anything like it. I've seen him go after drunks trying to grab my tits, or cheats, or white guys thinking they can wear a gun into the casino. He can take them down without breaking a sweat. On their faces, cuffs, that's that. What he did to you was personal."

Sigh. "I'm not proud of what I did. I don't know why I did it, now that I've had some time to reconsider. It felt right at the moment." He shook his head. "I probably should go straight to jail when we get back. Drop me off. I'll take my chances."

"It can't be that bad."

If there was ever going to be a chance to get this girl off his crotch. "Look, I shot a guy."

"You what?"

"I killed him. I shot a guy, I killed him." Slow Bear took a sip of coffee. That right there, an ending. A period on the mess. Then he said, "He'd just killed a couple of other people."

"Why?"

"One was an accident. The other was her husband. Maybe they were both accidents. Maybe he felt good squeezing the trigger, but then as soon as he'd done it, you know, he felt bad. Maybe I should've left it at that."

If he'd expected her to be afraid, it didn't work. She looked curious. But of course he couldn't just say I killed a guy without explaining why. He didn't want her to hate him after all, just not like him so much.

She said, "You're still a cop. Still fighting crime."

"A cop would've arrested him."

"About fifty-fifty, wouldn't you say?"

He nodded. Almost out of coffee. "Yeah, okay. Fifty-fifty. But he wasn't dangerous. He was just…scared by that point. He didn't even know I was going to shoot him. That's the shame. But he threatened me first. Told me he was taking me down with him."

The server was a guy with big hoops in his ears and a nose stud. Bald by choice. He poured more coffee and asked if they needed anything. Slow Bear shook his head but Lady wanted a slice of raspberry pie.

Slow Bear thought about what he'd done. Was she right? Was he just doing what any cop would've done? Why risk it? Because he was no longer a cop? Because he wouldn't have been able to hold Vlad there with only one hand until the real police showed up? Because he didn't really want to be involved, period?

Or was it because Vlad had done gone and pissed him off and that's how fucked Slow Bear was in the head? It was perfectly justifiable, or would've been in 1875.

"I thought you didn't drink coffee," Lady said. She'd already gotten her pie. Slow Bear hadn't noticed the guy bring it.

"I tried to give it up. But I need the caffeine."

"Then why did you try—"

"Heroin. I gave it up because of heroin."

Her eyes widened, her lips got tight. "You do heroin?"

A deep breath and sigh and fuck fuck fuck. "I used to. Once I lost my arm, they put me on some pretty lame pain pills, but I didn't like them. I got OxyContin instead. I liked those. And next, someone offered heroin, and I tried it, and I really liked that. But shit, heroin, girl, that's a lifestyle choice. That's a commitment. So I kicked it cold-turkey twice. Three times. And that got me onto coffee, which was a much better replacement than I expected. So I was making six, seven pots of coffee a day. But then I ran out of money. Coffee is expensive."

"So is heroin."

"So is orange juice. But I like orange juice. I like coffee. I'll just drink cheaper coffee."

"It's free at the casino."

He grinned. "I'll remember that. Is that pie good?"

"Shit yeah," with her mouth full. She cut off a bite with the fork and handed it over.

He ate the bite and agreed, that was some good fucking pie.

After paying for breakfast, gas for the car, forty-eight cans of Coors Light and a CD she insisted on by a guy named Pitbull, they had three-hundred-nineteen dollars and two nickels and four pennies left. And after a couple more tries at hotels with cash in hand, they decided that even though there were vacancies and they could afford the room, they'd rather split the cash and spend it on something better back home.

But first, Lady wanted to dance.

"Take me dancing. Someplace a little dirty."

"It's not even noon."

"Yeah, okay, we'll have the place to ourselves."

"You sure you wouldn't rather go home?"

She grooved with her shoulders. "If we go back, I'll get called into work. It always happens. I got called into work one time after I called in sick."

"How'd that happen?"

"I wasn't really sick. Someone saw me laying out in my mom's yard. So I had to go to work. Eyes everywhere on the rez."

Slow Bear stared out the window. Last time he'd been here it was just as crowded, just as chaotic, but the mood had been different. Back then, they were still on the upswing. Now, the oil industry was in decline. The men who'd banked on it had nowhere to go yet. Plus, all that money wasted on the high cost of living—rents, booze, dope, steaks. Women, so much money wasted on women, just to have a woman to talk to, to stare at, to reach for, to grope and laugh with, yeah, lots of money spent on women. The women had moved on. The strippers, anyway. There would always be Vegas, Florida, L.A.

These sad-sacks out on their asses? The guys who spent six months learning a job that was only going to do them any good out here? The smart guys who realized the money was in renting equipment to the oil guys, but now were stuck with huge lots of trucks and platforms, neglected, rusting away? The franchise owners opening all the fast food joints these guys had back home? The immigrant families opening liquor stores to keep these guys nice and lubricated?

Could they all afford to wait it out?

From the looks of it, no, but they were going to try anyway.

In the meantime, block after block of lounging oilmen, eating fast food sandwiches and drinking from brown paper bags. A lot of CLOSED signs in empty businesses.

"Dancing. Sure. We can try it."

She clapped and the car swerved right towards the curb.

Slow Bear grabbed the wheel with his only hand and Lady clasped hers on top of his. "I need to fix that."

"Jesus!" He was breathing hard.

"Are you really going to dance? I don't mean slow dance. I want to have fun."

He let go of the wheel, tugged his fingers from under hers, and collapsed into the seat. "I know the place."

They parked a lot closer than he'd ever been able to before, back in the boom times. Right across the street from El Norte Revolucion which was for the Hispanics and the Indians and the other darker-hued peoples. They worked the same fields as the whites, side-by-side every shift, but were persona non grata at the mostly white strip clubs, now shut down. What the whites didn't know was that El Norte Revolucion still had their basement—topless and bottomless, every night, all shades, full bushes welcome—and didn't give a damn about regulations.

Of course, on a busy boom night the first floor might as well have been an orgy. The crowds, man. Backslapping compadres from the fields, barmaids sweating through their t-shirts to get beer and tequila and tacos in as many hands as possible while the stereo system played Mexican narco tunes or American rap or speaker-rattling flamenco guitar. Grinding dancers and drunks made out in bathroom stalls while other couples pounded on the doors for their turns.

In the boom times.

This afternoon the sunlight only lit a few feet of the entrance before giving up. Slow Bear plunged right into the haze, the darkness, because standing there letting your eyes adjust showed you were a newbie and thus a target, and Lady grabbed hold of Slow Bear's shirt to keep from being left behind.

Like he remembered. Long, narrow bar on the left ran two-thirds of the length, the cheapness of its original construction now covered over with more wood, black paint, a brass rail along the bottom. Haphazard collection of bottles in front of a variety of thrift store mirrors. Hardly enough room between the stools along the bar and the booths along the right side to squeeze by without turning yourself sideways. The booths, probably salvaged from a Denny's. A hookah on every table.

In the back, the digital jukebox and the dance floor. Eight-by-eight, but when it was hopping it felt infinite.

Two men at the bar, youngish, both giving Lady the once-over. Both taking deep breaths and turning back to their drinks.

Slow Bear slid into the last booth, facing the door and the two guys. The whole joint smelled like mildew, stale beer and cumin. He lifted his hand and snapped his fingers. Lady's lips were parted, like O. Mah. Gawd. Not her scene. Not her scene at all. Slow Bear pulled the hookah menu from behind the stem and handed it to her. "Ever smoked one of these?"

"Maybe my grandparents did. Man!"

"Let's split a bowl, how about it."

"I don't smoke."

"It's mostly weed. The tobacco is for flavor."

She shrank back a little. "I don't know."

The barmaid who came over was, of course, too young, too distracted—texty, texty—and too bored. "Yeah?"

"Bring tacos, all the meats, for both of us until we're done. Keep them coming. And orange juice. And whatever she wants."

Lady ordered Mountain Dew and chips with salsa. And Slow Bear saw her eyeing the hookah list.

"Come on, tell her what you want."

"What do you want?"

Slow Bear grinned. "Go on."

She ordered blueberry. Slow Bear added, "Make it a special," which is what you said when you wanted it mostly weed. The bar girl, already turning, said, "We don't do special anymore."

She walked away. Slow Bear said to her back, "You kidding me?"

Idiot.

He looked around. They'd added more posters to the walls, mostly movies. Looked like they weren't too discerning—Beverly Hills Chihuahua?—and all sorts of blown-up photos of guys on the oil fields, goofing off, doing the hard work. Bunch of panties were draped over the top row of bottles that had never been opened and never would be.

One of the guys at the bar slid off his stool, headed towards them, and plopped down by Lady. This Indian was rough—shaved head, scarred, some fuzz coming back. Three eyebrow piercings. A green zombie hand, the ink vibrant and new, reached from under his work shirt up his neck, spread its fingers across his scalp, ear, and cheek. When he smiled, you could hear his teeth vibrate.

"You wanted a special?"

"Used to be on the menu."

"So did the egg and bean burrito, but enough people got sick." He turned to Lady, eyes all over her chest. "Hi there."

Slow Bear said, "So, the special?"

Zombie Hand ignored him. "My name's Gull."

Lady laughed. "No it's not."

"No, seriously. Gull. Like the bird"

"Man, you got what we need?" Slow Bear pulled out some of the leftover money. "How much?"

"Gull, right? More like ghoul." Lady flirty, trying to make Slow Bear jealous?

The barmaid showed back up with chips and salsa and drinks. She said to Gull, "They want a special."

"I heard them. Why you think I'm here?"

"To hook up with Fat Tits, seems to me." Poor barmaid had herself a crush.

Lady laughed again. "That's okay. Maybe yours will grow in soon enough, child."

Her and Gull laughed and that made Slow Bear lighten up even though this guy, Jesus, fucking loser this guy. The barmaid held up her middle finger and let it hang in the wind while Lady beamed at her. As the barmaid walked away, Gull shouted, "Now don't go spit in their tacos, bitch!"

She probably would. Slow Bear didn't care. He and Gull got down to business, but Gull wanted to stay and smoke with them. Lady was cool with that. Shit judge of character. She'd proven that twice now. So why was he feeling like a dad wanting to scare away some bum his daughter had dragged home?

They smoked a bowl and Slow Bear stopped hating on the little tweaker so much. He even told the story about how he lost his arm. Ho boy. Slow Bear almost died, but he didn't. Pretty much everyone else involved did. At least the asshole who shot his arm off died. That was enough.

Then Slow Bear recovered, retired with disability, and spent most of his time playing detective at the casino, or sitting on top of his trailer, his beloved Richardson Bi-Level trailer, watching the stars.

But the two kids across from him got bored at that part and were talking about their own world, this Gull guy going on about wild parties, about shows he'd seen out on the West Coast, names of bands and rappers Slow Bear had never heard of, right? And these kids, they had no problem talking about sex, right out in the open. Him about crazy exes, because the pierced, tattooed guy always had crazy exes, like, blowjobs while she held some scissors, or PCP fueled threesomes that were as scary as they were erotic.

And Lady was making shit up, Slow Bear knew she was. No way she'd got her boyfriend to blow a cop to get out of a ticket, and no way she'd dated a circus clown who always wanted to fuck in full make-up. Hell, he was impressed with her being quick like that. But he also realized, other than the fact that blueberry mixed with weed tasted awful, that Gull probably wasn't telling the truth, either. Why had he automatically assumed he was?

Slow Bear thought he was going to end up ignored after a while, as the place started to fill up, the lights above grew stronger, the music on the box went louder and a few hardy bastards fresh off work put on some narco tunes and performed for the others. But then the music switched over, all about that bass, bout that bass, and Lady smiled big, told Gull to let her out.

She stood and reached down for Slow Bear's hand. "You said we'd dance!"

"You were going to dance."

"We both were. Come on."

He was about to say no again when he caught Gull checking out Lady's boobs from the side this time, and thought, If not me, then him. "You're right. Yeah. Let's do this. Let's go."

It started with them kind of bouncing, swinging their arms. Lady even did "The Swim," but mostly they laughed. Slow Bear kept checking back through the dancers and the fruity hookah haze to their table, Gull still there smoking their bowl, watching Lady. There were about ten empty plastic baskets that had held three tacos each. Slow Bear was feeling the weight of them now—chorizo, carne asada, lengua, chicken, and some unlabeled hot sauce that gave him a fever.

The songs switched, and they eventually leaned in to each other, slow dancing to a song that was too fast. He needed her then. He held on for dear life with his one arm. They swayed. He closed his eyes. He felt her let out a deep breath against his neck, and this time when he looked back at the table, the tweaker Gull was gone. Off selling more specials, Slow Bear supposed.

"Come on," he told Lady. "Time to go."

"Yeah, you're right." She yawned. "Closing time."

Slow Bear checked his phone for the time. "No. It's seven-fifteen."

A big smile. "Damn, that was special, wasn't it?"

CHAPTER 6

Wasn't either of them going to be able to drive back to the rez that night, but one of them still had to drive back to the Walmart parking lot so they could sleep it off. Goddamn, that Gull wasn't selling no stems. No weak-ass shit. Slow Bear didn't know if this was really Lady's first time to get high or not—hazarding a guess, he'd say no—but it was most certainly her first time to get high on primo weed, and it showed. She drove like an old person, hunched close to the wheel and keeping it at a steady twenty-eight miles per hour.

"It's so big."

"What?"

"The car," she said. "It's weird. I try to push my car around with my hands—" She mimed pressing against the steering wheel with her palms. "—Nothing! But in here, I barely move a muscle—"

"It's the engine."

"That's heavy, too."

At least she wasn't giggling. If Lady had turned out to be the type that giggled, he might have hitched his way home.

He was already thinking, in the spinning car with the spinning world around his spinning head, about what to do next. Maybe show up at his cousin's office, explain that Santana was too smart for him, sussed out his real reason for showing up. Which was kinda true, except for the sussing out part.

After that, he was free to head back to the trailer, and ask its forgiveness for his sins. He would recalibrate his moral compass and enjoy the starlight. Maybe get himself a real telescope, finally. No, not that. Sure, it made one thing bigger, but you had to shut one eye and squinch the other one right up to the eyehole and hold your breath to keep it from shaking. He liked the way he was doing it already, both eyes wide open and seeing all things bigger across the sky as the seasons changed and the Earth spun (like his head was spinning, but faster), training his eyes to pick up the faintest stars and gas clouds and comets and supernovae.

Back in their parking spot, him and Lady talked about how weird they felt, and she admitted she thought Gull was kind of cute—not her type, but she liked the attention. He'd had no chance she said, spitting it out like old gum. No chance at all. He began to wonder if it was such a bad thing after all, if she really wanted to be with him, to try it. Not all the time, of course. Not constantly. He was still too PTSD for that arm-shot-off thing. But not a one-night stand, either. It wouldn't be fair to her, Slow Bear reasoned, to play with her feelings for him. Rather, he should indulge them. I mean, look at her, slipping off her jeans again and pulling the windbreaker over her as if you'd seen her mostly naked for a long time now, like a boyfriend. She was comfortable. She made Slow Bear comfortable, too.

So, yeah. Yeah.

But not in this fucking car. Fuck that. He would wait until the drive home, talk to her about it, let them get someplace with a bed, or a shower, or even a couch. He'd go see his cousin after. This was more important.

Slow Bear wasn't getting deep sleep, because he kept waking to her chubby cheeks only inches from his, her taco and blueberry breath, and because he couldn't stop spinning. He got out and forgot where he was and wandered to the back of the car, pissed all over the back bumper, getting splashback. He then had to dig for some fast food napkins to wipe it off before climbing back in, Lady pretending to sleep but obviously trying to stifle a laugh. He wished she wouldn't.

"Go ahead," he said.

And she did, and it was like geese honking, but he loved it.

That's when some motherfuckers smashed her window, stabbed the inside unlock button, and opened her door, too

49

fast for spinny-headed Slow Bear to react. It didn't matter, because there were two on his side as well, yanking open the door to pull him out and drop him to the asphalt and kick him in the back.

Lady squealed. Slow Bear got his bearings before the next kid tried to kick him again. Another two guys with both Lady's arms dragged her backwards toward a Toyota Pathfinder (remember), silver (remember). He tucked and rolled away from the kicker and got to his feet, ready to chase after, when the second guy clocked him with an aluminum bat right across his shoulders. Damn thing rang like he'd dinged a homer. Call it the numbing effect of good weed, tacos, and trying to save a lady in distress, but he surged ahead. The Pathfinder was another ten yards away. A veritable first down.

Slow Bear tried to squirm the pain from his back and shoulders while running, but it caught up with him. Lady was still squealing from inside the SUV, calling his name, before the man next to her wrapped an arm around her, covered her mouth. The SUV growled and lurched forward. Slow Bear tried to run in front of it, but it was too quick. He slammed into the side and tripped, nearly fell under the tires, covered his head with his arm. The SUV swerved and missed.

The kid with the bat gave him one more punishing swing, right across his fucking shin, before the friend yelled, "We out! We out!" And they ran off towards a motocross bike, mounted it and spun gravel back at Slow Bear.

Pulsing pain, the parking lot spinning out of control, he closed his eyes and thought of one thing: the guy wrapping his arm around Lady had a motherfucking green zombie hand tattooed on his motherfucking face.

He did his best to get a move on, go after the cocksuckers, but the pain from getting his shit kicked and from his own bad judgment had him seeing triple.

When he'd finally shaken that off, he went right back to El Norte Revolucion and banged on the door. Joint was closed, but that didn't mean the bartenders and their friends weren't in there getting freebies. He thought he heard one shout (over some choice Public Enemy from back in the day), "Knock one more time and we'll fuck you the fuck up, motherfucker!"

So he went around back, kicked the door in.

The bartenders and their friends had guns.

But none of those friends were Zombie Hand.

"I want the guy with the neck tattoo," Slow Bear told them anyway. "The zombie hand. He took my friend."

"No idea who you're talking about." The bartender held a cheap shotgun on him. Cheap didn't matter. "But I want you to notice something. Not a one of us is bothering to call the police. You see that?"

Slow Bear scanned the room. A line of men and women in various states of dress—mostly undress—doing some karaoke and crystal and booze while grooving to Chuck D's anger, most of them now pointing some, he guessed, legally-purchased weaponry in his direction. The only two without guns was a bartender lying flat on her back on the bar, texting someone, and a little dude in a booth, hands shoved deep in his pockets.

Six guns. Six fucking guns, man. One, two, three…

"Listen, I don't want to cause more trouble than I have to, but all you've got to do is give me a name, an address, anything that'll get me out of your party and on my way."

"Hey, I know you." The girl on the bar. Long black hair. Squid ink sheen. She propped onto her elbows, one knee up and her other ankle dangling. Flip-flops and dirty feet. "You were that rez cop. Yeah, you took some weed off me one time, busted my boyfriend's nose. Laughed at him."

He shrugged. "Maybe."

Oh, shit, he remembered her now. When he got home after the shift, he'd jacked off thinking about her.

Her friends now gave him the stink eye. "He's a cop?"

"Like, back on the rez, not here. I don't think he's a cop anymore, not after he lost his arm. Now he sits around the casino, drinking. Sad."

"Wait, you know me? Then you know Lady, right? Works

at the casino? Bartender?"

If there was a chill of recognition, she covered it right quick. "Who?"

"My friend, her name is, her name is…" Shit, remember! This was important. "Kylie. Her name is Kylie. Someone took her."

One of the guys with the guns laughed. Sounded mean. "You keep telling yourself that. She probably was dying to get away from you."

Slow Bear ignored him, walked past all the people with the guns to the girl. "Seriously. If you know something—"

"Hey, Canine!" Not quite a shout. Stared him down while she spoke. "He's getting a little too friendly. Get him out of here."

Canine was a big fucker and looked like he'd been summoned of fire in a Mexican jungle rather than born. He wrapped his arm around Slow Bear's waist from behind, picked him up as if he was made of packing peanuts.

Slow Bear kicked, hit him. "Please!" Eyes on the bartender. "Please! Anything you can tell me!"

She shook her head, eased back onto the bar, and went right to texting again. "Fresh bacon, Canine. Eat up."

So Canine took Slow Bear out back, dropped him into the dumpster, then slapped him about his head and neck while the others laughed and smoked and threw beer bottles at him. None of them broke, but they all fucking hurt.

When they got bored with that, they went back inside, leaving Slow Bear to crawl out of the dumpster and lay in the dirt for a while until the pain subsided enough for him to go back to the car, climb in, and cry.

Because, fuck, he had something to cry about.

Next morning, Slow Bear sat outside Santana's office with the motor running, heater on high now that Lady's car had a broken window. He waited hours in the parking lot, in plain sight. The security guys saw him, let him know they were watching, but he stared ahead, paid them no mind. Then a couple of dark sedans pulled up on either side of the car, tinted windows. Back-up, he supposed, but he didn't give them the pleasure. Just stayed put, motor on, pebbles of glass under his feet and his ass, crunchy when he squirmed.

Soon enough, some others pulled into the lot. A couple gals, couple guys, and the one called Waterbug–June, that was her name. Like Carter Cash. Like the month when lots of people got married. Her and her staff, and eventually the Fed Ex guy and the DHL guy both, stood out there watching. Smoking, watching, laughing, smoking more.

Slow Bear stayed put. He knew this was a long game. Longer than baseball.

Another dark SUV with tinted windows pulled up alongside the sedan on Slow Bear's left. The guy who climbed down from the passenger seat—Manfred, tough guy from yesterday—stopped to speak with the sedan's driver before lifting up, patting the top of the car, and walking over to Slow Bear's busted window hole. Standing tall at first, looking in all directions but at Slow Bear.

"How about you leave?"

"How about you tell your boss I need to speak with him?"

Manfred took the same pose he had at the sedan: leaning, hand on roof, hand in pocket, still not really looking at Slow Bear. "I would say we can call the police, but let's not. It would be much more fun to sic these dogs in the cars on you."

"Real dogs?"

"Fucking idiot. No, not real dogs. But you'll wish they had been by the time they get done with blunt objects and sharp-toed boots all over you."

Slow Bear shook his head. "I need to see Santana again. It's urgent."

"That's not an option."

"It's the only option."

Manfred kept staring, on through Lady's car and into the next car and maybe beyond that to the dusty plains covering his deep crude paycheck. "Mr. Bear, what exactly woud you say to Mr. Santana if given the opportunity to speak with him again? Hm? Can I relay a message?"

"Nope. Face to face. None of your goddamned business."

"I see, I see." Fingers tapped up top, onetwothreefour. Five. Onetwothreefour. Five.

Slow Bear waited him out. Nothing to say. Not a word. Manfred was paid to be a cowcatcher, pretty much. But sometimes the thing to worry about wasn't on the tracks.

So Manfred sighed again, rose to full height and pulled up his pants by his belt. The windows on both sedans lowered by about an inch. Slow Bear caught two sets of angry eyes staring at him from each one. The bodyguard moseyed on back to the SUV, climbed back up, and Slow Bear got a quick peek inside when he opened the door.

Santana was the one driving.

Well, goddamn.

Slow Bear didn't think. He opened his door and left it open as he rounded the sedan, the SUV, and parked himself in front of the driver's window, tapping on the glass with his knuckles before two of the dogs from the sedan had gotten to him and put him in an armlock/headlock combo and dragged him back about five feet.

Forearm on the back of his neck. Dust getting into his eyes. Good view of the ground, and a whole lot of pain all over.

The driver's window slid down some.

Santana's voice. "Boy, does he have a gun?"

"We don't know."

"Can you check for a gun?"

The 'boys' gave him a rough once over, more than once on his raw bits. "No sir, no gun."

"Then let the man go! What's he gonna do? Punch me? One-armed man is going to punch me in the face? Jesus. Son?"

The boys kept a tight grip. Goddamn them.

"I said son and I mean Mr. Pokey Bear or whatever your-"

"Slow Bear, you piece of shit."

That got him headlocked tighter.

"I SAID LET HIM GO!"

The dogs on either side released him, and Slow Bear did a spin around like he was going to launch at one or the other of them. Made him dizzy. Then he stopped spinning and found the SUV again. Santana's eyes peeking out over tinted glass, a stream of freezing air gushing out. Slow Bear stepped closer, heard the dogs seethe, Sssssssss you better watch it.

Santana lowered the window some more, until his nose showed. "I thought our business was concluded."

"It was. I changed my mind."

"About what?"

"About the job offer."

Santana laughed. Turned to Manfred. Manfred laughed. Santana laughed louder. Then back to Slow Bear. Big smile, big smile.

"Wasn't no offer. Wasn't no offer about it."

Slow Bear nodded. "Okay."

"Okay?"

"Can I have a job, then?"

Santana stared at Slow Bear for a long time, or at least it seemed like a long time. More people had showed up to watch and the dogs were crawling closer, breathing down Slow Bear's neck. But then the window slid all the way down with that little whine and Santana was smiling.

"Sure. We can do that."

Manfred stopped smiling.

"Thank you, sir. Thank you very much." Slow Bear nodded. "Now, I need a few days off first."

CHAPTER 7

Back in Santana's office, another glacier's worth of cold air tumbling forth from the vents, drying out Slow Bear's sweat until his skin was like onion paper, the three men–Slow Bear, Manfred, and Santana, along with two of the eight dog-men– had an interesting conversation about what exactly the fuck Slow Bear was going on about.

"Stole her?"

"Bashed in the window and dragged her away, kicking and screaming. I didn't have a chance."

"And what about the bar?"

Slow Bear sighed. So slow to connect the dot, these guys. "I tried to find out who it was that took her, but the people at the bar gave me shit. Knocked me around. But they know. I know they know. I have to go back and ask less nicely."

"How does that have anything to do with me giving you a job?"

"You got guns?"

"Maybe."

"I'd like some."

Santana's eyes widened, but not so much in surprise as sheer joy. Slow Bear was a delight! Crazy-assed son of a bitch expected Santana would hire him, hand him guns, and let him go off on a vendetta.

Manfred tapped his fingers on his armrest. Onetwothreefour. Five. Slow Bear turned to him. "Knock that shit off."

Santana laughed, rolled his chair closer to the desk and set his elbows down, fingers intertwined. "Sex trafficking."

"Excuse me?"

"Girls getting themselves in all sorts of trouble, either

shipped in from overseas, or over the border, or owing on some dope, heroin, meth. Some out-and-out sold by fucked-up parents. Out here is the wild goddamned west. You think Deadwood is the frontier? Shit, Deadwood is a casino resort town for retirees now. You're sitting in frontier central right here. Williston might as well be Saigon during the war. Or, or, like, New York back in its scummy days. If someone took your girl like that, and she was a wonderful creature, indeed, well, I'm afraid they won't let her go easily. And certainly not to a wasted one-armed Indian."

Slow Bear grinned. It was bad. "Sober me up and point me in the right direction."

Santana stood, held out his hand. It was the wrong one. Slow Bear shook anyway. "I'll do you one better. Me and Manfred will go with you. Five arms are better than one."

Half an hour later, El Norte Revolucion was bathed in the blood of idiots. Santana and Manfred did not fuck around. Some of the same fuckers who had given Slow Bear a hard time were now lying on the floor, coughing, wheezing. The girl with the squid ink hair, Manfred had slapped her around a bit, too. Busted her lip.

Shit, even Canine, the bastard who'd tossed Slow Bear in the dumpster, was picking up one of his teeth from a puddle of bloody spit.

Blood on Santana's boots. On his dress slacks. On his fists and shirt. None on his hat, though. That hat, Jesus, what a hat. Gray Stetson. No wonder The Hat was so envious.

One of the idiots gave up the name of Zombie Hand pretty quickly: Gull Pompedeaux from East Texas. Originally was "Gilligan," thanks to his waste of a mother. Shortened to "Gil" which became "Gull."

The rest of the beatings were just to make sure.

Slow Bear didn't have to do much of anything but guard the back door. A few times he got to point a pistol at one of them trying to escape, including squid ink girl, sending them back into the fray with a shake of his head.

When it was over and done with, Santana went up to another bartender, the only one who'd escaped the beatings, and ordered a round for the entire bar. "And it had better be mescal."

A shot of mescal later, everyone apologized to Santana and Manfred and, shit, even Slow Bear for the trouble they'd caused, and the squid ink girl—Melinda—grabbed a mop and bucket and started sloshing the blood from the floor in her filthy bare feet.

Santana leaned on the bar. "Problem is, one of those assholes is going to call Mr. Zombie Hand Pompedeaux as soon as they hit the sunlight and let him know we're looking for him. I don't expect that's going to help."

"You think he'll run? Take Lady with him?"

"Aw, shit no, he's already rid himself of the girl. The whole point there was to get a payday. But we need him to tell us—"

"Got it. Where he sold her—"

Santana's free hand swung up and slapped Slow Bear on the ear. "Don't interrupt me boy. Pretending like you got there first. You kidding me?"

"Sorry sir." The gun was itchy in Slow Bear's waistband. But no, it wasn't going to be like that. "You're right, sir."

Santana turned to Manfred. "Remind me to dock him a couple bucks for that one."

CHAPTER 8

Gull Pompedeaux lived on the top floor of a fairly new apartment building with an already broken elevator because the whole thing was built for oilmen who got drunk a lot and tried to destroy everything around them that didn't give them a paycheck. From the outside, with the patches of dirt and the unpainted walls, it looked as if the workmen got it up to "move in" standards and then said "Fuck it."

In the stairwell: stains of beer, puke, blood.

The smell of food gone bad.

Guys shouting.

SHIT!

FUCK!

GODDAMNED MOTHERFUCKERS!

All in the distance somewhere, but still too close for comfort. Slow Bear winced every time another one bellowed forth. He was sandwiched between Santana, taking the lead, and Manfred, always a step too close to Slow Bear's back. He felt as if he was being pushed up the stairs.

Up top, the door to the hallway was missing, replaced by a duct-taped shower curtain. No reason to ask why. Again: oilmen. They flicked aside the plastic barrier and walked down the hall. Most of the doors were steel. Scarred and dented. At least half the numbers were missing but Santana figured out which one they wanted, stopped in front of it–Slow Bear wishing Manfred would get off his back already–and pounded on it with the side of his fist.

"Gull Pompedeaux! Wake up! Gull Fucking Pompedeaux! You clump of cat shit, you!"

The white guy who opened the door, kind of chubby and shirtless, blinking into the light, was not Gull Pompedeaux.

"The fuck?"

Then his eyes went wide. "Mister Santana, sir."

"That's more like it. May we come in? Of course we can. I'm going to help myself to your water, too, because that was quite a climb–" And on and on he went, right through the door, followed by Slow Bear and Manfred.

The big man closed the door after them, didn't try to stop Santana. All the big man wore was a pair of baggy shorts, hung real low. Mouth open to catch flies. They all filed into the kitchen, an unholy mess of dirty dishes, empty takeout bags, beer bottles, Bacardi bottles, Coke cans. Santana looked through some cabinets, found a cleanish plastic cup, and went to the fridge. There was a gallon of spring water inside. He poured a glass, gulped it down.

Santana: "–Where are my manners, though? Winston, meet my associate Manfred, and this one-armed fellow is Micah Cross."

"Slow Bear."

"You sure are. So, we're here looking for your roommate."

Open mouth. Blank.

"You know, the man you share this apartment with."

Open mouth. Blank.

But then Winston said, "What about him?"

"I'm looking for him. Seems he snatched a person of great importance to Mister Bear here, and we can't have that. I need to make sure Mister Bear's lady friend is being treated well."

Winston shrugged. "Why don't you just–"

Santana was on him like electricity, grabbing his jaw, making his mouth look fishy. "What was that? Are you being smart with me, boy?"

"No sir! No sir! Absolutely not!"

Santana let go, gave him a light double-tap on his cheek. "Good. Now. When was the last time you saw him."

"I don't know. I don't keep up with him."

"Not necessarily the last time he was here. What do you remember as the last time you saw him?"

Shifty. "A couple days ago?"

"You sure?"

"Yeah?"

"Was he alone?" Slow Bear asked.

Winston turned to him. His face went mean. "Fuck you."

Santana gave him a harder slap this time. "Hey, that's my friend. You will give him all due respect. Was Mister Zombie Hand alone?"

"Who?"

"Gull, you bag of filth. Gull!"

"I'm getting a little tired of this shit. Here I was, catching up on Instagram, some pictures from my girlfriends, and I got to deal with you?"

Santana pinched the bridge of his nose. "Manfred? Take care of this?"

Manfred took out what looked like brass knuckles–Jesus, people still had those?–grabbed Winston's right arm, and start beating the crap out of the big man's elbow. Over and over, the brass-on-bone sounding crunchy. Winston screamed, tried to get away, but Manfred had a hold and he followed Winston every frantic step around the living room until he collapsed to the floor crying, his elbow gone to mush.

"He was alone oh god shit he was he was alone motherfuck fuck FUCK fuck please, please, no more, he was alone, I swear I swear–"

"Admit it," Santana said. "You don't have any girlfriends."

"I don't, I don't, I don't have anyone!"

"Where's Gull?"

"He's gone, man, gone, I don't know where, I have no idea, please."

"One more time. You said he was alone. Was he alone?"

"No, he had some fat chick with him. Fat Indian girl. That's all I know. That's it. I'm done!"

Winston cradled his mangled arm, then Santana looked it over, clucked his tongue. "This doesn't look so good. Oughta take that down to the Emergency Room."

Winston shook his head, crying. "It'll be alright. I'm good."

Santana pulled out his wallet. "Nonsense, boy. Here, what

do you think, about five hundred? Is that what an ER visit runs these days?"

Slow Bear was about to speak up, tell him no, it's much more than that, when Winston said, "I'll take it, I'll go to the ER."

As if he was a child, this overgrown idiot. Jerking off to Instagram shots, somehow rooming with Pompedeaux.

"Okay. So go on, now." Santana gave him a shoo with his hand. Winston nodded, grabbed his keys and took off out of the apartment.

Once he was gone, Manfred and Santana had a nice laugh and helped themselves to more of Winston's water. They offered some to Slow Bear, who said no in spite of his dry mouth. The older men settled onto Winston's couch, a paused video game on the TV screen and Winston's abandoned cell phone between the cushions. Slow Bear remained standing.

"Well, you heard the man," Santana said over his shoulder. "Gull's gone. Girl's gone. Now, we can hunt him down. Might be slow. Might take weeks. In the meantime, I've got some work I need you to do for me."

"I've got a job. Finding Kylie is my job."

"Young man, did you hear a word I said? We'll find her. You owe me something else, though, and you better believe I get what I'm owed."

They both took hearty gulps of cold water.

Slow Bear stayed still and quiet. What sort of jobs? What had he gotten himself into? And where the fuck was Lady?

"Let's go back to the office. I'll start hitting up my contacts while you clean yourself up a little. Don't want you representing me looking like some methhead."

Did he really look that bad? This whole trip had drained the life out of him. He followed Santana and Manfred out of the apartment, still wondering what was happening and why he couldn't catch up.

CHAPTER 9

Back at the office, Santana showed Slow Bear his executive bathroom—or 'shitrocm' as the boss called it. It was nice and warm, with toilet, sink, and a walk-in shower. Thick towels. Santana told him to get himself clean and they'd see about getting him some decent clothes. Clean ones, anyway. Santana buzzed June out in the front room, told her to get Mister Bear's sizes and pick up something at the fleet store.

Slow Bear locked the bathroom door and stopped in the buzzy silence. Closed his eyes. Calm, please. He reached out for the sink but the room kept right on spinning for another minute or two. That might have even been a tear in his eye, but he was so pissed off it evaporated from the heat.

He got the shower temp right and shed his clothes. Now that his head had settled, he could tell why Santana was so insistent. Slow Bear smelled like a garbage buffet, something pigs would like. Layers of filth. He climbed in and the hot water hit him like a heroin rush. Good God. For a moment he almost forgot he had only one arm, and he imagined himself running his hands through his hair. For the longest time he stood still and let the water beat him senseless. He watched dirt run off him, swirl around the drain.

After that, he lathered up, his muscles crying out. Too many days of sitting at the bar, sitting on his trailer. Not enough doing things like walking or lifting heavy things. He'd really let himself go since the shooting. It wasn't the best condition to go chasing Lady's captors, but it would have to do.

Rinsed off. Dreaded turning off the water, but he did it anyway. Toweled off and then wrapped it around his waist. Thought about taking his old clothes with him, but fuck it. He'd wander around in a towel.

He must have been in the shower a hell of a long time because when he walked out of the bathroom a bag from the fleet store waited. Carhartt jeans, a Wrangler western shirt with flowers sewn on it, gray socks and a box of CAT work boots. Tighty-whiteys.

The new clothes stuck to his skin after the hot shower. The sleeves on the shirt were too long–ha, ha–but he would worry about that later. The jeans were snug, the seam on his crotch cutting his balls in two. The boots were fine. Surprised she didn't buy him a hat. He stepped back into the bathroom and dug his trucker cap out of the pile of discards. It smelled like eggs-from-hell, but he set it on his head and pulled down the bill.

Then he walked out to Santana standing with a couple of men in real suits and ties. Jolly laughs and handshakes all around. Manfred stood by the door, hands tucked behind his back. Slow Bear didn't make himself known. He just leaned against the wall and waited. Eventually, the suits looked at him a little funny and their jollies turned into nervous giggles. Santana didn't bother introducing them.

"Gentlemen, my next appointment is here. Thanks for coming."

Manfred took over and ushered them out.

Slow Bear strolled to the desk, slumped in one of the chairs. Legs out in front, elbow on the armrest. "You got something for me to do?"

Santana sat on the front corner of his desk, as if Slow Bear didn't deserve proper business meeting manners. "Sit up straight, boy, before I get Manfred to do it for you."

Motherfucker. So now Slow Bear got it. He'd done sold his soul to the devil in order to do the right thing. He pushed himself with his boots, slow, until his back was straight as a battleship hull. "Better?"

Santana growled low in his throat.

"Sorry."

Santana nodded. "So let me explain what I need from you. Time to time, some of the boys on the Bakken get into a little

64

trouble paying what they owe."

"Bills?"

"No, listen. Lots of them pay for things they don't get receipts for, if you know what I mean."

Slow Bear hoped he didn't know, but probably did. Shit.

"Couple of things, especially. Now, when they do run into trouble over this, they sometimes come to me, ask if I can help out. And I do. I do. I'm happy to. But there has to be something in it for me. Otherwise I'd be a broken ATM, just jizzing money all over the place. With me so far?"

"So far."

"Now it's double jeopardy. They got out of the first trouble, but they somehow think they can put me off easier. Maybe because they think I'm a rich man and don't need it so much as they do. If that were true, I'd never have become rich. I ain't a pushover, son. I only let them go so far. That's where you come in." He extended his hand, as if Slow Bear was on display at a museum. "You, my friend, are their reminder."

"Reminder?"

"You remind them they owe me. You remind them hard and loud. You make them clearly remember how much they promised to pay me back, with interest, and how long it's been. A very simple job, I'd say, something your previous career certainly qualifies you for."

Quiet in the room.

Slow Bear understood. He didn't want any part of it, but he understood.

"I'm a one-armed man."

"Who has already shown me he can take care of himself."

"Are you fucking serious? Look at me. I'm a disaster."

"On the outside. But I think you can handle chumps who have a lot to lose if they don't pay up."

"Blackmail?"

Santana smiled, and his whole face wrinkled into a rotten jack-o-lantern. "Collateral."

Slow Bear shook his head. Then he thought about Lady sleeping beside him. Then her screams as she was being

65

dragged from the car. Then how nobody came to help, not a single damn one of them oilmen camping out in the Walmart parking lot. Like they hadn't heard a thing.

Slow Bear let out a long breath. He'd give it up as his last if that meant Lady could go free. But that wasn't going to do it.

"Fine. Give me the name."

CHAPTER 10

The noise was goddamned unpleasant. The chemical odor was worse. The flat dirt stretched beneath them all. Far underground, the roughnecks were blowing up hard-packed soil, making it bleed oil and sucking it all up. Fracking. Slow Bear wondered what the terrain would look like once they'd done sucked it dry. Would it crumble away, sinkholes everywhere? Would there be earthquakes all over North Dakota like there were in Texas now?

Slow Bear didn't have any more time to think about it. He had the name, the company name, and the location, so here he was in a lifted jacket and hardhat. Sleeve still flopping around. Like it mattered. He didn't need to put on the ruse for too long. Find this man, remind him of his debt, and get out.

He walked through the field with its trucks and tubes and steel and mud. Held a clipboard to make him seem official. No guns, though. Santana told him to leave it on the desk. Off by the road, a long line of trucks waited to be filled with crude oil so they could drive it to refineries, force it into gasoline. Liquid money. Couldn't hear a damned thing over the compressors. Had to stop and ask lots of guys if they knew where to find Tracker Hall. Tracker. Fucker was legally named Tracker.

These guys didn't want to talk to him. Fine. Slow Bear didn't want to talk to them any more than he had to for the job so he could get back to searching for Lady. He might have a few rounds left in him after all.

So he looked around for dark faces and hands. Asked them to point out Tracker Hall for him. Got only slightly more help than from the whites, but it was enough. Soon he tramped through the mud towards a group of roughnecks shooting the shit, laughing, smoking, all turning to him once one of the hardhats lifted his eyes and saw Slow Bear waiting.

"Yeah?" A fat hardhat.

"Which one's Tracker Hall?"

They all traded glances. There was this one kid, had to be in his twenties, who crossed his arms and flexed his back. Grinned. Big bastard. "Who wants to know, Chief?"

Oh, how they laughed.

Fat one: "Chief Bear-Ate-Arm."

Another, pockmarked to hell and back: "Chief One-Hand-Whack." Mimed jerking off. Slow Bear thinking, What, you use both?

He said, "Look, I don't give a shit about any of you except Tracker. And I only care about him because Santana told me—"

Didn't even let him finish. The big bastard took off, heading deeper into the field. Slow Bear chased after, lucky to avoid getting tripped by the head hardhat–leapt right over the fat fucker's leg–and gave it his all. The air was on fire. He sucked in flame after flame, let out smoke, felt like. He wasn't losing the kid, but he wasn't gaining either.

A ruckus behind him. He stole a glance. Chased by a whole horde of hardhats.

Aw, for the love of…

He poured it on. The kid was dodging and weaving pipes and tubes and trucks and this was getting ridiculous. Slow Bear was finally closing. No idea how.

The horde behind him dropped back, but it wouldn't take them long to catch up.

Slow Bear tried to get the lay of the land ahead of him, ahead of the kid. He cut left out of the maze and ran a straight line. Shins splinting, feet like broken rocks, holding his breath.

Looked over.

Almost caught up.

They were near the edge of the field where a line of trucks

blocked both of them. The kid turned right, going to keep on running. Slow Bear had no choice, but he was damn near running on empty. Over his shoulder, the horde had amassed an army of grunting ogres.

Up ahead of the big bastard, a truck door yawned open too late for the kid to adjust, and it nearly took his head off. The impact like a gunshot, echoing across the oil field. Knocked him back onto the ground. The driver leaned out and looked down.

Slow Bear caught up and dropped to his knees beside Tracker Hall, who was rolling and groaning, hands covering his face. Slow Bear shut his eyes tight hoping the world would stop spinning, tried to get his breath back. Before he could do that, he was surrounded by the angry horde of hardhats, steel-toe boots stomping. He opened his eyes. A sea of jumpsuits. Two of them grabbed Slow Bear from behind, one wrenching his arm and the other holding him around his chest. He fought but was too tired to get free. Another few went to Tracker's side.

They forced his hands away from his face. Squirming. The boy's nose was flat and bloodied. His eye socket was broken. He was inconsolable.

The horde turned their eyes to Slow Bear.

Who said, "Didn't I tell you I work for Santana? Let me go!"

They did. Slow Bear wasn't ready for it. He fell face first. Felt like something new was going to bruise. Anyway, he picked himself up, slapped dust off his jeans, and stepped over to Tracker, looked down at him.

"You owe Mr. Santana some money."

If he could hear, the kid didn't show it. Still rolling around. Bawling now.

Slow Bear nodded. "Yeah, so, anyway, make sure you get him some money, okay?"

He turned to the horde, lifted his hand high. "You saw it yourselves. I never touched him. All I did was deliver a message."

He waited for someone to break the silence. Maybe he expected someone to point and shout Let's get him! And that would've been a real bad day, about as bad as any he'd been having after getting his ass kicked off the rez. Once they take home away from you, what's the worst anyone else could do?

Thus, he walked. He walked right up to the wall of ogres in hardhats. He'd take them all on if need be.

But the closer he got, they started to part. Red Sea, man. Hard stares, but no balled up fists. No wrenches ready to come down on his skull. He kept his head moving, left to right, behind and ahead, but he realized they weren't going to do anything. He had the magic word. Santana.

He made it back to the car unharmed. He thought back to Tracker Hall on the ground—the bones in his face obviously broken. The kid would look like a Cro-Magnon for a long while to come.

Looked out at the field, noticed a couple of security guards in the distance, watching him. He waved. They didn't.

Slow Bear cranked up. All this over a loan? Kid willing to run that far and fast over a simple loan? How much did he borrow?

Enough.

The only answer that mattered.

Slow Bear nodded and drove away.

CHAPTER 11

It was well after midnight, and the heat was still unbearable Stuck in some sort of high pressure system. High pressure al around. The temps made people lazy, but it also made them hateful. Slow Bear had made his way around to all the bars looking for a lead. Where were the whores? How did a man get his cock sucked around here? He used to know, back in his cop days, but it seemed all the rules had changed in just over a year.

Strip clubs: gone.

Streetwalkers: gone.

Pimps: out of sight.

He'd sit in bars and pay close attention to what was going on, but he was getting dagger-eyes in return. He would nurse two way-overpriced light beers, "Indian Happy Hour" said one of the white chick bartenders, and keep his eyes and ears open. When he tried to take a sip, someone would bump him from behind. Daring him to get pissed off about it.

He didn't think asking any of them "Where the whores at?" would help him get into their good graces.

So, watching and listening, that was all he had.

Bar number three, beer number six, and he wasn't hearing so clearly no more. He wasn't seeing hard edges, either. He should've switched to orange juice a few drinks back, but that would've really made him stand out. As it was, he was lucky no one had picked a real fight with him yet.

Slow Bear turned his stool facing the rest of the place so he could try to figure out the prostitution rental and distribution system. Hell, if he could find one. A glance at the clock over the bar. It was still early, bar time. He needed to keep himself awake.

From behind him, a voice: "Buy you a drink, kemo sabe?"

The air around Slow Bear felt suddenly colder. He turned his head to find Manfred standing there, too close for comfort.

Slow Bear tightened his grip on the beer glass. "You got it backwards. Kemo sabe was not the Indian."

"Hell, I know that. I was being ironic. Buy you another?"

"Orange juice and vodka. Without the vodka."

Manfred clapped Slow Bear on the shoulder and laughed. "Just for that, double the vodka."

He called the bartender over and ordered. She gave Manfred a smile and instant service. How about that? Slow Bear tasted the drink. Alcohol fumes up his nose. What a hot mess.

Manfred pushed the barstool next to Slow Bear's out of the way and leaned against the bar rail. Swirled the ice in his whiskey. "Staying out of trouble?"

"What fun is that?"

"Well, you've got a job now. First time in a long while you've had to punch a clock. Don't want to get in bad with the boss so soon."

Slow Bear scrunched up his eyes like, What? "I don't give a fuck what the boss thinks. It's not that kind of job."

"Tell yourself that. But when you're a poor man working for a rich one, they're all that kind of job. Am I right?"

"What do you want?"

An exaggerated shrug. "Just happened to be out and about. Just happened to see you sitting here all by your lonesome. Thought you could use the company."

Bullshit. Slow Bear knew exactly what this was. A reminder that his leash only went so far. He held up his drink. "Cheers."

Clink.

Manfred sipped his whiskey like he'd never had any before.

Slow Bear only pretended to sip his. No more.

Then they let the noise of the bar roll around them. Nobody jostled Slow Bear from behind anymore. Manfred showing up effectively killed his Lady-hunting for the night.

But didn't this also mean Manfred had probably been on his tail all evening? Knew what he was up to? Of course he knew what Slow Bear was up to. That was part of the deal. That didn't mean Santana wanted Slow Bear prowling around at night on his own. Never knew what he might stumble on.

"The boss got a call earlier." Manfred turned to watch the milling crowd. He elbowed the bar. "A friend of yours."

Slow Bear's heart sped up. "Kylie? Is she okay?"

Manfred shook his head. "No, no. I mean Tracker. Tracker Hall, remember? Didn't you go mess him up a little today?"

The moment replayed in his head, the kid slamming into the truck door. His face like a cracked window. "I didn't touch him."

"Hey, I'm no cop. Whatever happened, he's fucked up pretty good. Called the boss from the hospital. We could barely understand him. He said he'd pay up in a day or two. So I'd call that a success on your first day. Congrats."

That kid's face. It didn't feel like a victory. "How much?"

"What?"

"How much was he in for? I didn't think it was supposed to be much."

Manfred grinned. "How about leaving that to the accountants? Some things Mr. Santana likes to keep private."

Another clap on the back nearly sent vodka down Slow Bear's windpipe. It was bad enough already in his mouth. Keeping up appearances.

He'd had enough. "I appreciate the drink, but I'm all full up. I'd better get going."

"Come on, look at it. You barely touched the thing."

"Really, though."

"I can't let you leave it this way. It's rude."

"Why do you want me to drink the drink?"

"I bought it for you!"

Slow Bear slipped off the barstool. Took him a moment to find vertical. "I'm sorry. I don't want the drink."

"Sit back down." Swirled his ice. "Wait til I'm done, at least."

Slow Bear kept his hand on the stool, kept standing. "I'll stand here til you're done. Then I've got to go."

"Enjoy your drink."

"I don't want the drink."

Maybe it was just the shadows of the night, but something dark moved across Manfred's face. He grabbed the vodka and orange juice in his fist and dragged it closer to the edge of the bar. "Drink your fucking drink."

Slow Bear pointed at it. "I think you put something in my drink."

"What did you say?"

"I said I think you put something in my drink."

Manfred held himself straighter, taller. "What are you saying? I would drug you? You think I would drug you? Like I want to carry you home for a little fun? That kind of drug? Is that how you see me?"

Slow Bear blew out his cheeks. Oh boy. He eased back onto the barstool, eyes on Manfred the whole time, picked up his tumbler and took another sip. The ice had diluted the vodka a little, but it was still strong as all fuck.

Manfred smiled and went back to leaning. "See?"

"You're insane."

"But I won." He called the bartender over, asked for another whiskey. Got a wink and a smile. Slow Bear watched the bartender pour it. Canadian whiskey. She saw him watching and frowned. So he looked away.

Another minute or three went by. Manfred thanked the woman for the drink. Slow Bear heard her whisper, "None for him. He's cut off."

Fine. It wasn't about him. It was about her.

Then Manfred said, "Why her?"

Slow Bear turned back around. "Hm?"

"Why this girl of yours? What's so urgent about this?"

He let a beat go, thinking the dude had to be kidding. And another beat. But Manfred was serious. "You do know she was taken by force, right? Grabbed from her own car by fucking hooligans?"

"Okay, yeah, but why didn't you go to the police? Why are you out here looking for her alone? Or, I mean, with the boss' help? Why not call in the big guns?"

Going to the police had never occurred to Slow Bear. He was the police as far as he was concerned. "She's my friend."

"That would be even more reason to ask the cops for help. If you're serious about finding her, why wouldn't you? Because all you've done so far is let whoever has her off the hook. That's two days of searching they could've done."

Slow Bear shook his head. "She's my friend. The cops won't do anything. Got to do it myself."

"How do you know the cops won't do anything? Lots of girls out here. They've found quite a few runaways and kidnapped kids. I bet they have a lot of connections. So, what are you doing?"

Felt heat on his skin. "I'm doing the right thing."

A laugh. "Like fuck. You're being an asshole. There could be professionals on the trail right now instead of you hoping to stumble across her in a bar."

"I'll find her."

Manfred swirled his ice, stared down at it. "Out of your goddamned mind."

"You're supposed to be helping me."

"Sure, sure. I'm paid to. But I can still have my own opinion about it."

"I will find her. I swear."

Manfred shrugged. "If you say so."

Slow Bear pushed the drink away. It was still mostly full. "I've had it. I've got other places to be tonight."

"Still think you're going to find her in a bar?"

He slid off the stool. Woozy. He'd told himself he wouldn't let this happen, but damn it, just damn it.

"Because that's not how it works," Manfred went on. "You're barking up the wrong tree."

Slow Bear waved him off. Slow and slurry, "I'll bark up where I want. You don't know things."

"Where are you going to sleep tonight?"

Slow Bear held up the key to Lady's car. "My own RV."

"Not in your state."

"No, I'm good. I'm good."

Manfred tossed a twenty on the bar and clamped his arm around Slow Bear, gave him a squeeze.

It got hazy after that.

CHAPTER 12

Slow Bear woke up warm in a cold room. His eyes were too crusty to open, and his arm was cocooned so he couldn't reach up and wipe it off right away. He was under some sort of cover. He tried to push it away with his feet. Nothing budged.

Panic.

He pulled his hand free quick and shoved it out, tried to escape. Slid half his body out before realizing he was in a sleeping bag, zipped up nice and tight. He'd used his own rolled-up jeans for a pillow. The rest of his clothes were in a pile past his head. Boots too. He was still wearing his underwear though. For a moment, he wondered if this was Manfred's place, that the man had brought him home and had his way with Slow Bear after all. Yeah, there had to have been something in that drink.

But once he'd rubbed the crust from his eyes and adjusted for the dimness, Slow Bear realized he was back in Santana's front office. It was gray outside, the light of day only a hint so far. Those big windows. He'd been exposed here while he slept. On display like in a zoo.

Goosebumps. The air was on full blast and it felt wrong to Slow Bear, who'd gotten used to sleeping with his windows open back home. Gotten used to the temperature of the natural world, his body adjusting to the changes of the seasons.

He stood at the window. Best guess, it was somewhere around five in the morning. In the distance, lights from the fields, lights from downtown Williston. But look away and all you saw was dark-as-pitch prairie.

Where was she out there? Was she okay? Had they beat her? Had they…

He wouldn't let himself think it. A twist in his guts started low and tightened. He clenched, steadied himself with his hand, flat on the glass. It left a sweaty, greasy print, sliding sideways.

He pictured Lady. She'd become his friend without him realizing it. It had happened at the bar, in that damned casino, and he was too stupid to know. Maybe he'd thought it was pity. And now, for an act of kindness she had thought might fill up a few hours on the road, she was gone.

No, she was in Hell.

He, in the meantime, was in a cozy office waking up after a decent handful of hours sleep.

Thought about what Manfred had said. Why hadn't Slow Bear gone to the cops? There had to be a better reason. Was he afraid of them? Now that he had no badge, was he afraid of the very people he used to cooperate with? Did he trust them, knowing the way they spoke about their jobs, the people they were supposed to protect, and the Indians who'd been here far longer than any of them could imagine?

Trust. What bullshit.

The only person he trusted anymore had been ripped away against her will and instead of doing the smart thing to get her back, Slow Bear had ventured forth like a goddamned Boy Scout trying to earn his hero badge.

Fragments of the previous night came back to him. Striking out at bars, Manfred finding him, plying him with a too-strong drink and some questions he couldn't really answer. Then Manfred leading him out, not letting him drive. They piled into one of Santana's big SUVs and drove back here, where Manfred set him up with a place to sleep.

No, the man didn't touch him inappropriately. He just rolled out the sleeping bag and told Slow Bear he was locking him in for the night.

Slow Bear walked over to the front door, tried it. Locked.

He walked to Santana's office door, tried it. Locked.

At least the bathroom door was open.

Still, Slow Bear couldn't help but piss in the potted plant

over by some of the guest chairs. It had to be done.

After that, he tried some of the drawers on Waterbug's desk. All were locked–although easily broken into if he'd wanted to–except for the top one, full of paperclips, pens, a letter opener, a spoon, blank post-it pads and rubber bands.

He went back to the sleeping bag, sat down on it.

Blinked away sadness and swallowed hard. He crawled back into the bag and curled into a tight ball.

He waited.

Must've fallen asleep again pretty quickly, because he was awakened by the office door flying open and smacking into the wall, someone whimpering. It was bright as fuck outside.

Slow Bear sat up and watched Manfred push a man ahead by the back of his neck. Santana was right behind them. The man was cowering, twisting his neck, which had a green zombie hand tattooed on it.

Santana circled round until he found Slow Bear, then smiled. "We got him."

Manfred sat Gull Pompedeaux in one of the chairs by the desk. Slow Bear stood, still in his undies, slowly stepped towards the punk, a wide arc. Not quite believing his eyes, not quite sure what to do.

Santana walked behind his desk, tossed his hat onto it, and ruffled his hair. "Okay, you wanted to talk to him, so talk to him."

Slow Bear stared, mouth agape. Gull's face was smashed. A purpled eye and a lip three times normal size. String of bloody drool. His left cheek looked like they'd taken a cheese grater to it.

"Jesus," Slow Bear said.

"Go on." Santana waved a hand at the dude. "Ask him. Gull Pompedeaux, tell him what you told me."

The man flinched, looked down at his lap. "Please, no more."

"Tell him."

"She's on a truck, probably heading out west. She's

probably loaded on smack. That's how we keep them under control."

Slow Bear crept closer, squatted down beside the chair until he was face to face. "Keep going."

"What? What? There's nothing more to say. This is what I do. She's going on the game. A few months from now, she'll forget her old life."

"Call the truck driver, get her off of there. I'll go pick her up."

Gull shook his head. It looked painful. "No, man, I can't do that. My, my boss, I don't have any control. Jesus, man, leave me be."

"Who's your boss? I'll go get him next."

Manfred slammed his fist into the side of Gull's head. "Tell him!"

"Stop!" Slow Bear stood, shoved Manfred back a step. "I want him in one piece, alright?"

Gull flicked his eyes between them, finally settling on Santana. "Why are you letting this happen? Please, just make it stop."

Santana crossed his fingers across his chest, leaned back. "I'm afraid it's out of my hands. The man wants answers, so we'll give him answers. What was the question?"

Slow Bear knelt again, his hand on the back of the chair this time. Closer. "Who's your boss?"

"I don't know."

"Liar."

"I don't know! I-I-I've got a lot of bosses."

"Tell me one of them, just one, and I'll take it from there."

There went the eyes again. Flick, flick, flick.

Sweat. Top of his head, running down his face.

"Come on," whispered Slow Bear. "My friend is in that truck, and you're the only one that can help me right now."

Gull squeezed his eyes shut. "No, no, no. I'm nothing. I'm nobody. I'm a tool, man, a tool."

"Tell me."

"I can't!"

"Tell me."

More sweat. Upper lip. Neck.

Teeth trembling. Tapping.

Then a tornado descended from behind him and whipped Gull away.

Not a tornado, but a Manfred. He yanked a plastic bag over Gull's head and pulled tight. Tighter. Tightest.

Pulled Gull right from the chair. He windmilled his arms. Kicked and thrashed, but Manfred had a steady hold on that bag.

Slow Bear had fallen on his ass when it happened, and now he was working to stand up, shouting, "Stop it! Stop! Wait, wait, he was going to tell me!"

Manfred, cheeks bright red, grunted, "No. Just another lie."

Gull kept struggling.

Slow Bear turned to Santana. "Please, make him stop."

Santana stood from the desk, crossed his arms. Looked like he was thinking about it. Watched his henchman asphyxiate this low-level whatever-he-was.

He said, "No, I've got to agree with Manfred on this one. Boy's a born fibber."

"You can't kill him!"

A nod.

Manfred let go and Gull dropped to the ground like a sack of rocks, rasping for breath.

"You're right, son. I can't kill him. But I can let Manfred go work on him awhile. Maybe that'll help break him down. Go on, get him out of here."

Before Slow Bear could protest, Manfred grabbed Gull by his neck again and led him out of the room fast.

The rasping faded. Nothing but the sound of the air conditioner swooshing and Waterbug's desk phone softly purring every now and then.

Santana sat again, an elbow on his desk as he stroked the bottom of his face, which looked harshly shaven. His skin was rawhide.

"Get yourself dressed, Mr. Bear. While Manfred is working

on your problem, I'll need you to do another job for me."

Slow Bear cringed. "Another man who owes you money?"

"What led you to believe there was only one? I've got plenty for you to do, don't you worry."

"I mean, is there anything else? Wash your car? Some laundry?"

Santana looked up, a little surprised. "I thought we had an understanding."

"Yeah, but—"

"We're not going to change our understanding because you feel a bit squishy about it. A job is a job. A deal is a deal."

"But...last time, um. About last time."

"I don't need to hear any more." Santana held up a blocking palm. "It's not pretty work, and you did what you had to do. You have my permission to do it again, if needed. Hammer the fucker's face in. Break his limbs. Tickle him too much if that's what it takes. Now, time's a wasting. And get dressed, I said. It's weird, you in your underwear."

Slow Bear covered his chest. Instinct. Dropped his hand to cover his junk. He felt good and damn well fucked.

CHAPTER 13

Another oilfield, another maze of hoses and trucks, churning wells, wires. A jet of fire in the distance. Tanks bunched together off to Slow Bear's right. He'd been told today's man was somewhere in the midst, but there wasn't anyone around. Not at first glance. He wondered if the site had been shut down. There was a trailer to check first.

It was like a boxier version of an airstream, painted blue with panels of stainless steel at the front and over the doors. The truck that hauled it in was long gone, as the trailer looked like it had been here forever, coated with dust, dirt and a sheer of oil. Multicolored splotches in the sun. The company name was painted across the side. Very professionally done.

Slow Bear climbed the steps and opened the door. No point knocking.

He interrupted a group of five men stood around chatting, laughing, who all looked at him at once. There were cheap desks, old computers, a water cooler, a coffee-maker and a microwave in addition to the filing cabinets. Smelled like burnt popcorn and stale coffee.

These guys weren't roughnecks. They were middle-management. They wore either dress shirts with loose ties and a name tag, or a beige pullover polo with the company logo. All white. Of course they were.

"Help you, sir?"

This from a man too old for the soul patch he was wearing and too young for his beer gut. The others varied in age—thirties to sixties. Slow Bear wondered how many of them were carrying guns.

Just like he was.

"I'm looking for Braden Jarvis. One of you him?"

They all looked at Braden Jarvis. That's how Slow Bear knew which one was Braden Jarvis. Not even a one of them could hold out.

Jarvis was five foot something and one hundred something. No facial hair. Looked like he had a receding hairline a few years too soon. One of the ones wearing a polo.

But it was a man with thick gray hair, a plain blue tie and a nametag that said H. Fuller stepped away from the group, close to Slow Bear.

"You come looking for him at work? During business hours?"

"I thought so, yeah."

"And what gives you the right to come down here like judge, jury, and executioner?"

Slow Bear thumbed over his shoulder. "The door was open."

The men formed a line between Slow Bear and Jarvis.

"What's all this about?" H. Fuller said.

They knew. Word about Tracker's accident must've spread quickly. Slow Bear thought about the gun shoved into his back waistband. Thought about how long it would take to get it out and if that was enough time. Thought about the trouble he'd be in if he had to pull it.

Dead or in jail. Dead or in jail.

"Santana sent me."

The magic words worked before. But they didn't have much impact now. The line closed ranks. Like a brick wall.

"So?"

"So I've got business to discuss. Could you gentlemen please give us the room?"

Nothing.

Couple of them crossed arms.

Slow Bear took a step back. Was it time to pull the piece yet? He didn't think so. Wait, now, just wait.

The Soul Patch Man swaggered over. Sure, he was fat, but he was thick. Slow Bear figured he could take a punch, throw a punch, and make someone hurt.

Slow Bear didn't want to be that someone.

Soul Patch Man was a few inches away. "Listen, son." Breath like onions and mustard. "You don't belong here. Tell this Santana that you can't get all up in a man's workplace over something personal like this."

He waddled forward, forcing Slow Bear back.

"Listen–"

Back back back.

"Seriously." Slow Bear peered over Soul Patch Man's shoulder, making eye-contact with Jarvis. "Maybe we can talk outside for a minute."

Soul Patch Man's gut was doing the pushing now as Slow Bear was almost to the door. Slow Bear didn't even have room to grab the gun if he wanted to. The man reached past him, opened the door, and shoved him outside. Slow Bear fell off the steps and landed butt-first on the ground. A bad jolt.

Soul Patch Man sneered down at him, then slammed the door.

The dust he'd kicked up made Slow Bear cough. He was still hurting from Trevor kicking his ass only, what, a couple days ago. Was that all?

Those guys, like jackals in there. Slow Bear could hear the laughter through the thin trailer wall. Santana must've been off his gourd thinking Slow Bear could handle this job. Stupid job, anyway. He felt like a mob enforcer.

Oh, God, that's all he was, wasn't he?

Santana was running more than some "loans" to "help a few guys out." This was serious green.

Alright, then. If that's the way Santana saw him, then that's the way he'd act.

Looked back across the lot at Lady's shitty little import. No, that wouldn't do. That wouldn't do at all.

So he went hunting through the grounds, climbing into the cabs of empty trucks, flipping the visors down, checking the center console for keys. Had to be some lazy men here.

He found it on the fourth try. Not one of the monsters that hauled the oil or towed the equipment. This was a modest

Dodge 3500 that had held up well under artillery, it looked like. Okay. Another slow three-sixty, make sure he could get away with it.

Nobody.

Slow Bear opened the door. For a truck that was beaten and filthy on the outside, the owner did a fine job of keeping the cab spic and span. Even had a coconut air freshener. He slipped into the driver's seat, cranked up, and pulled onto the dirt path he'd just come from. A left. Another left. There was Lady's car. There was the trailer he'd been thrown out of.

He sped up and drove right the hell into it.

Boom, baby. Jolted him harder than the ground had, but at least this thing had shock absorbers.

The trailer crumpled like a Coke can. He got out to inspect the damage, still feeling like his entire body was a funny bone that had been smacked one too many times. Still, he was up, alive, and a little proud of himself for what he'd done.

He'd taken out the door and the steps, so he had to hop on his hood, then hop across a chasm to get back into the trailer, where the men who'd been mighty confident of themselves not ten minutes earlier had now been knocked the fuck out.

Well, okay, at least they'd been knocked down. Wasn't none of them dead, anyway. That was luck on his side.

What if he had killed one of these bastards?

Hmm. Hadn't thought of that.

Chilled him a tiny bit. But only a tiny bit. What was life worth anyway? Everyone trying to hold on to it, cherish it, only to realize far too late, after too many visits to church and empty prayers, it's a thing like any other thing. It's dirty. It sucks. It ends badly.

Slow Bear cleared some debris and rolled the men over, one-by-one. The floor beneath him felt loose, every step bouncy as if nothing was holding it up, as if it might collapse at any second. He turned over Soul Patch Man, who was groaning. Looked like his leg was bent the wrong way. Looked like he might have lost an eye. Slow Bear kicked him back onto his face.

There was Jarvis, tangled under a chair beneath his broken and overturned desk. Slow Bear flicked the shitty particleboard away, knelt beside Jarvis, and shook him back to consciousness. He'd come through with some scratches and probably some bruises.

"Hi, I'm Micah Cross. I work for Santana, and he told me to remind you about that loan you owe on."

"Jesus, man."

"Do you understand?"

Jarvis sat up and looked around. "What have you done?"

Slow Bear snapped his fingers in front of Jarvis' face. "I'm over here."

"My God."

"How much are we talking here anyway? A few grand? It can't be more than that, can it?"

Jarvis finally looked him in the eye. "That's...it's not like that. You don't know?"

"Enlighten me."

"He sends you here and you don't even know."

The other men were starting to stir. Slow Bear was out of time. "Just tell me already." He pulled his pistol. "I was hoping I wouldn't have to—"

"It's not money, you asshole. It's product. I owe him for product. I...he gave me some cocaine and I paid for some of it but not for all of it. I owed him after I sold some. But I didn't sell enough, okay? I owe him because I didn't sell enough cocaine. We got carried away. We used it up."

Slow Bear facepalmed himself. It really was that simple, but he was too stupid or too crazed or too rattled to have seen it. Of course Santana was a drug dealer. Of course he was.

Jarvis went on, "And I'd racked up a tab at the Mile High Club."

Slow Bear spread his fingers, peaked between them. "A bar?"

"Jesus, you really don't know—"

H. Fuller was standing now, stretching, growling, "Fuck!" Blood trickled out of his ears, his nose. He looked around. He found Slow Bear. He started over.

Slow Bear hopped back onto his feet and swung the gun around towards Fuller. "Hold up." Looked back down at Jarvis. "What is it? The Mile High Club? Tell me."

"Man, it's…it's a club. A sex club. No, okay, it's like, a brothel. Okay? They let me have a few freebies over there, but they weren't really free. So now, shit. Shit. What am I gonna do?"

"A sex club?"

"Didn't I say that?"

"Owned by Santana?"

Jarvis shook his head. "I don't know, man, but it sure seems like it. He was always there when I was. Him or this guy who worked for him."

Manfred. Slow Bear said, "Yeah, I know him."

"The guy with the wicked tattoo?"

Whoa.

Slow Bear blinked. "What tattoo?"

"You can't miss it. The zombie hand on his neck?"

Slow Bear almost pulled his trigger from the shock. H. Fuller would've been a goner. But he caught himself in time.

Sirens coming. Closer every second.

Didn't matter. Let them throw him in jail. Because if they didn't do that, Slow Bear was ready to kill a couple sons a bitches.

CHAPTER 14

Slow Bear sat in a cell for three hours. One of those concrete bunker-style rooms. They didn't have the iron bars any more. The door was solid and thick like a bank vault. Luckily it was still early in the day and the only other guys in here were sleeping drunks from the night before. Except for one big white guy giving him the staredown, a sense of explosive violence under the surface.

Slow Bear didn't need that shit today. Or any day. His body was still shook up from crashing into the trailer. And the other beatings he'd gotten before that. How much abuse could a human body take? Did he have undetected internal bleeding? Hairline fractures that would split more with each jolt? A concussion?

Maybe it was like what happened to blind people who got a sharper sense of hearing. After losing his arm, maybe the rest of his body toughened up to prevent something like that happening again. Didn't mean he was invincible. Just meant he could take a lot of hurt. Sure, he felt every fucking moment of it but he was still standing.

No, he was sitting. His ass was sore after three hours on cold concrete in a cell that smelled like piss, whiskey, and farts. Four drunk men's fart brands mixing together in the air to create something witches might brew.

At least they came for the big white man first. Even as he walked out the door, he kept the stink eye on Slow Bear. What was that about? Maybe Slow Bear had hassled him before when he had a badge. Maybe the fucker was a racist.

Then they came for a couple of the drunks. Had to wake them, practically drag them to their feet. One of them said, "Jus' a few—a few more—few more hours."

They had a free phone in the cell to make calls. Slow Bear made one to Waterbug soon as he was thrown in here. She'd said she would get the message to Santana, but what was taking so goddamn long? Unless Santana wasn't going to bother getting him out of here. Did Jarvis get to him first? Told him what he'd told Slow Bear? That would be awkward. Santana had a lot to answer to, but Slow Bear wanted to face him on his own terms.

Santana had known from the start. Shit, most likely, he was the one who had ordered they take Lady. All this mess, running around doing errands for Santana while he helped look for Lady, all a fucking ruse. Yeah, if Santana already knew what Slow Bear knew, he might leave him here to rot. Pretend he never knew the guy. He was at a severe disadvantage. No contest. Public defender. Prejudice from the jury of his "peers." Jesus.

Another hour crept by.

He wondered if he could use what he knew to turn the tables. Tell the police about the Mile High Club. Tell them about the shit The Hat said Santana had done.

It wouldn't help. A poor one-armed washout versus a self-made businessman who gave a lot of people jobs in this town. No go.

The bunker door opened again and a cop guided in a filthy tweaker with an unruly beard and a poncho. The smell coming off him, Jesus, it covered up the farts and left pure human rot in its place. Slow Bear was about to object when the guard at the door called over, "Cross. You're out."

Oh what sweet relief. But who was on the other side waiting for him?

It was Manfred. Of course Santana wouldn't lower himself to the task. The henchman would do. It didn't help that Manfred was a grinning fool watching Slow Bear get discharged. Might as well be naked on a tightrope.

After, in the SUV, Manfred said, "We need to talk to you about subtlety."

90

"I'm more a shock and awe guy."

"Look where that landed you. Now you owe the boss your bail. You can work it off."

"What? There are more guys behind on payments?"

"More than you might think. It's a growth industry."

Silence.

Outside, midafternoon heat shimmered the highway ahead. They passed plenty of trucks on their way out of town, hauling oil to refineries around the country. When would the fields dry out? When would all this go bust?

Nobody thought about that out here. They only cared about the boom.

Slow Bear couldn't bottle it up.

"Take me to the Mile High Club."

Manfred turned his head. "The what?"

"You know what I'm talking about. No bullshit."

"I'm sorry, Micah, but I really don't—"

"Jarvis told me about it."

"Did he?"

"Take me to the club. I want to see for myself."

Manfred turned back to the road. "I don't think that's a good idea. The boss would like to see you now, anyway."

"I don't want to see him right now." Boiling over. "So tell me about how you took Pompedeaux away for what he had coming to him. You didn't do a goddamn thing to him, did you?"

"Did I forget to tell you you're getting a promotion?"

"I am not."

"Well, I wouldn't rule it out. Let's go back to the office."

How fast were they going? Under forty? Slow Bear opened the door. The wind blew it closed. He tried again and used his leg to prop it out.

Manfred slowed, trying to grab Slow Bear by the shirt, the belt, anything. Slow Bear squirmed away and jumped out of the truck, still going about twenty, and flopped hard, rolled over. Jesus that hurt! Like his neck was made of porcelain. Oh man.

The plan had been to hop out and start running. He'd find Jarvis again, or another one of these fools, and find the Mile High Club without help from Santana, which wasn't coming anyway. He couldn't imagine the man now without red horns sticking through his hat. Pitchfork in hand.

That was the plan, but it fell through the moment his foot touched the ground and twisted and sent him slamming into the hard packed dirt on the side of the road. Now, staring at the sky, he imagined the Santana Satan laughing and pointing down at him.

Soon, though, it was Manfred, leaning over, hands on knees. Blurry. There were three of him and they all said, "What the hell was that?"

"You... you lied to me. You guys had her all along. Let me go on believing you didn't know where she was." Trying to talk and push himself away from Manfred at the same time. A lot of effort. His ankles weren't broken or sprained, but they sure as fuck hurt when Slow Bear stabbed his heels into the ground and kept pushing. "Fucking liars."

Manfred stood straight and sighed. Crossed his arms. "What're you doing to yourself? You think I'm going to hurt you?"

Another shove away. Another flash of pain. He gave up. Flopped where he was, arms and legs outstretched. "Whatever. Leave me alone. Just leave me be."

Manfred shrugged and stepped away. Slow Bear waited for the SUV to start-up and drive away, but it didn't. Instead, he heard Manfred mumbling. He lifted his head just enough to see the man pacing, talking on his phone.

Thought he heard Manfred say, "He knows."

Thought he heard him say, "–rid of him? What else–"

"Mm hm."

"Okay, boss."

Then there was Manfred hovering above him again, reaching down to grab his arm. "Come on. You want to see the club, I'll show you the club."

Slow Bear pulled back some, but he was weak and aching.

"No, man, I heard you on the phone. You're trying to get rid of me."

"You're out of your mind. Get up and get in the truck."

"I'm not crazy. I heard you clear as day."

"You hit your head. You're all mixed up."

"Jesus, no!"

But all it took was a mighty pull and Slow Bear was back on his feet, trying hard to slip out of Manfred's grasp but not strong enough. He gave up, let the man walk him to the truck. Manfred brushed the dust and dirt off Slow Bear's back.

Why did he let himself be led back? Was he that out of it?

He wondered, though, if Lady might be at this Mile High Club. If so, he was taking her out of there alive, even if it killed him.

The ride over was quiet except for the low burble of AM radio. Sounded like a farm report. Slow Bear stared at the flat prairie passing outside, oil field machinery cluttering the view. He wished he was back on top of his trailer, staring out across the rez, nothing manmade in his sightline for miles and miles. He wished he had never gotten involved in a love triangle, wished he'd never gotten beat to shit by Trevor, and wished he hadn't woken up to Lady driving him to Williston. Just an all-around fucked-up chain of events.

It was all his fault.

You think?

"If you'd gone to the police, Micah." Manfred shook his head. "If you'd only done that, we wouldn't be here now. I told the boss it was a bad idea letting you bounce around town, gunned up and pissed off. But he thought we could get some use out of you that way."

"Motherfucker."

"And you are effective, I'll give you that. A bit over the top, but effective nonetheless. Still, now that you've found out about the club, there's no way to uncheck that box. What a shame."

"But you don't think the police would help? If I'd gone to them, like you said? You're so sure about that?"

He hur-hured it away. "Because they work for us."

Slow Bear swallowed hard. The dust he'd breathed in earlier scratched his throat. He had never gotten the impression that the cops here were bought, but he hadn't stumbled across something like this before. "I don't believe you."

"It doesn't matter if you do or don't. It's too late. Sit back, relax, enjoy the rest of the ride."

In the distance, an airfield. Nothing major. A place for cropdusters and other small planes to take off. Pretty bleak, actually. A small terminal. A long chain link fence that seemed to stretch forever. Some hangars. Manfred pulled off here. There wasn't a nightclub in sight. Slow Bear felt a cold ache growing in his stomach.

They zig-zagged around tiny prop planes and a couple jets, including a larger Gulfstream that must have belonged to one of the oil bigwigs. They drove between hangers until they came to one that was three times as large as the others. Even larger than the terminal. Manfred stopped outside it.

"Here we are."

"This is not a nightclub."

"Never said that it was. Come on, I'll show you."

There was another SUV pulled up there, plus several other cars. The giant doors were closed. Manfred got out and Slow Bear followed him to the smaller side door. As soon as they approached the door opened, held by a young man in a suit but no tie. Nothing bad happened as they passed through. No ambush. No guns. Nothing.

It was a small, dimly lit office. A dark-haired woman of about forty sat at a desk, iPad in front of her hooked up to one of those mobile credit card readers. She wore a tight mini-dress and smiled at Manfred as he stepped inside. He nodded. "Jessie."

"Manny. They're waiting for you." She waved towards a door that lead into the main hangar.

The man who had been tending the door now fell in behind Slow Bear. They followed Manfred through to...well, calling it the Mile High Club was starting to make sense.

Row after row of small airplanes, Cessnas and Beechcraft, wings overlapping. Two of them were rocking on their wheels. Squeaking. One had fogged windows, a footprint. Moans and grunting coming from inside.

There was also a helicopter without blades. In the front seat, for all to see, a couple. The woman naked and straddled on a man in the pilot's chair, also naked except for a flight helmet. Nearby, a G4 private jet. On the far end of the hangar, half the fuselage of a 737, still painted in America West colors, turquoise and orange.

Manfred kept on. Slow Bear was trying to take it all in. The guard slapped a hand on Slow Bear's shoulder, gave him a push forward. Okay, fine, not going to fight it. Plus, there were guards stationed all around the hangar, so he had nowhere else to go.

In the middle of the hanger, several rows of seats that must've once been in different planes. Relaxing in each seat were reasonably lovely women, a wide range of ages and sizes, showing off an awful lot of skin. A sickly sweet blend of body washes and perfumes curdled Slow Bear's stomach.

They all looked at him with dull, sleepy eyes.

Amongst them, standing tall, was Santana, resplendent in his black hat, black leather jacket, crisp white shirt, jeans and boots. Zombie Hand Pompedeaux right by his side. He'd taken his licks for show, and now he dared to smirk in Slow Bear's direction.

Another push from the guy behind him.

Slow Bear stepped closer. Santana tossed his arms open wide, as if he might wrap Slow Bear into a big hug. But he didn't. Dropped them at his sides.

"Micah, you stupid son of a bitch."

Slow Bear looked at the girls. Redheads, blondes, brunettes. Blacks, whites, Hispanics, Indians, Asians. Thin, curvy, obese. Some young as, God, he didn't want to guess, but sixteen? Some in their forties and fifties. All looking at him with Mona Lisa faces.

"Mile High Club, eh? Cute."

"Don't judge me, son. All I do is provide opportunities. If a man wants to get his jollies on a plane, even if it's on the ground, well, at least it's something different, am I right?"

"And these women? Forced to work for you?"

Big smile. "I see, I see, we're going to throw around some unfounded accusations? Is that what we've sunken to?"

The silence stretched.

Slow Bear spit on the ground by Santana's boots.

Santana got in real close to Slow Bear's face, dropped his voice. "Be nice."

"Where's my friend? Where's Kylie?"

"Oh yes, that girl of yours."

"She's not mine."

"You sure act like she is."

"Goddamn you."

"Sweet talker. Let's say maybe, maybe, she found herself in a particularly unfortunate situation. One where she didn't have the same amount of...control, yes, control over what happened to her as these ladies here. These ladies, they owe me money, or they owe me something. They are working off their debts. However, others might not fit into that particular niche. I said I make opportunities, and your girl was an opportunity indeed. I knew exactly the place she'd fit in."

Slow Bear balled his fist. Trembling.

Santana went on. "I don't see the world as people. I only see it as opportunities. She was one, you were one, these women here are one."

"If you hurt her—"

He pulled his face back, stared into Slow Bear's eyes. "You won't do a goddamn thing. Don't you get it? Listen, I'll tell you what we did—restrained her, probably bruised her some, but that'll heal. Injected her with some powerful sedatives, one of which, over time, she'll grow to love. More than herself, more than any other person, she'll grow to love that drug. She'll do anything to have it. So we'll tell her what she has to do to get it. See? Well, not us, I guess. That duty will pass along to the man who paid me for her and the others. My work is done."

Rip his throat out with your teeth.

Tear his nuts off with your bare hand. Shove them into his gaping throat wound.

"Santana—"

"Most of my employees call me 'sir.' But since I'm about to fire you, I'll let it slide."

"Where is she?" Through gritted teeth. Louder than he expected. He heard it echo back. "Where is she?"

"I put her on a truck, sent it down to Albuquerque. From there, I have no idea."

"How can you…Jesus. Like a piece of meat!"

"Like an opportunity. You're not listening. She came along at the right place and time. She filled one of our needs. We took her, then hoped you would tell the police and just go home. But I forgot you were a cop once. I forgot the story about how you lost that arm, trying to play hero. So along you came, barreling back into my presence, presenting me with yet another opportunity."

Santana reached out and grabbed Slow Bear by the chin, gave it a hardy wag.

"You were in love, weren't you? She gave you a reason to play hero. She was some quixotic quest for you, not a goddamned living and breathing human being!"

He removed his hand, but landed a slap across Slow Bear's cheek as he walked away, chest puffed out, circling his prey like an eagle over a bunny.

"So I used you. I could've easily sent Manfred to scare some of my debtors into paying what they owe, but you played your own role perfectly. Why waste a good opportunity."

"Stop saying opportunity."

"Did I tell you to speak?"

"Opportunity, opportunity, opp-or-tun-ee-tee."

"Boy—" Finger wagging.

"What? You're going to kill me? I kind of figured that out already."

He already knew he would never leave this hangar alive.

Scared the hell out of him, but he didn't want to go out weak. On the verge of tears. Thinking about himself back home, sitting on top of his trailer, two armed and happy again. An illusion. He thought about Lady–call her by her real name now–Kylie, scared, alone and drugged on a truck to another city where she would be enslaved, like so many other women, treated as possessions instead of real people.

He was going to die. It wasn't fair. He felt like a failure. He imagined what nothingness felt like.

When no one else answered him, Slow Bear said, "Get on with it. I'm done. No more Bond villain crap. Just…" He shrugged.

Santana sighed. "You disappoint me. I wanted to see you fight. I might have even offered you the services of a lady in any plane you like. A last request, say. But no, you're too dumb to play along. The windmills finally fought back, Quixote."

He waved towards his men. Manfred slipped behind Slow Bear and wrapped an arm around him, while the guard from the door lifted something–a syringe?–and started towards him.

"Micah, we looked into you, and one thing that everyone agreed on is that quite recently you were a filthy junkie. That's a verifiable fact. So, while shooting you and having to get rid of your body might be quite a hassle for us, we figure that letting the police do their job would be the easiest way to go. With all the homeless men roaming around Williston, all you'll be is another statistic, a junkie who overdosed in a stolen car in a Walmart parking lot."

The guard took Slow Bear's wrist. Slow Bear tried to pull away, but the guard held on. He clenched the syringe between his teeth while looking for a vein. Whatever strength Slow Bear had left in him seeped out from head to toe. He couldn't pull against Manfred. Too strong. All the abuse caught up with Slow Bear, as if his body wanted the cure for the pain.

A deep sense of longing for that shot of junk.

Sweet, sweet, sweet.

What a way to go. He wondered why it hadn't happened

sooner, why he hadn't topped himself, accidentally or not, when he was on the stuff. But something made him want to live. His shitty life was actually worth living. Then. Not now.

He willed his life to flash before his eyes, but it wouldn't. Old snapshot of Mom, old memory of Dad. The crazy man with the shotgun, pulling that trigger and blowing his arm off. Then, Kylie's laugh. Kylie's eyes. Kylie's…

The guard had found a spot. He took the syringe, slid it in–there was that familiar pinch–and plunged. The pressure giving way to…oh, Jesus.

How he'd missed it.

Into the sky.

Something wrong.

Of course there was something wrong. He was gonna OD.

Slow Bear laughed.

He sunk to the floor, Manfred and the Guard keeping him from dropping all the way.

His eyes tried to look up, up, up where he was floating, but he was looking down instead. Santana's boots.

"I can't imagine a better way to go, frankly. If it hadn't been you, it would've been someone else. And if it hadn't been your girl, well…what can I say?"

Slow Bear went Hmph. Managed to say, "Flipper."

"What's he mean, like the dolphin?" Manfred asked.

Slow Bear thought of a dolphin. Yeah, did he mean the dolphin? Did he mean anything?

"I don't care." Santana again. "Stick him in the jet until we're sure he's dead."

Okay.

He felt himself floating. On one side, an angel of mercy. On the other, a giant zombie hand from Hell. No idea where they could be taking him together.

No idea.

Nothing.

CHAPTER 15

Dead was like...

Hard to say. Slow Bear didn't realize when it had happened. If there was anything beyond the veil, he wasn't aware of it. Sure wasn't an afterlife.

There was nothing else.

Until he came back to life.

That was heat, building, building until he couldn't stand it. Then a gasp of breath.

Then Slow Bear sat up and started gasping, someone above shushing him. "They'll hear!"

Something in his mouth. Mushy. Vomit. He turned away from the voice and let the puke drain onto the floor. Tried to catch his breath, but it was raspy and thick. Hands fluttering on his shoulder and rib cage.

"Shh. Please. Shh."

This wasn't death. This hurt too bad to be death. He still felt numb and buzzed on the heroin, but all of his nerves were super-alert. Jangly.

He wiped his mouth on his sleeve and blinked until he found where the voice was coming from. A young woman, maybe not yet twenty, knelt beside him. She was wearing a sparkling silver mini-dress that looked too small for her, and she was rail thin. Her face pale and wiped clean of make-up, a smudge of lipstick the only trace, and flame-orange hair, curly, hanging over him.

"Are you okay?"

He blinked again and looked around. Airplane seats. He was in the middle aisle of a jet, flat on his back. But it was just him and this girl, no other passengers.

"Where are we? Are we flying?"

The girl shook her head. "We're in the club. The hanger. This is the jet."

His head started hurting. A real clamping, like King Kong had hold of his skull. "Ow, fuck."

"Quiet." A harsh whisper. She leaned even closer. "You have to hurry. They'll be back real soon."

"Who?"

"Gull and Manry."

"What?"

"They're coming to take you back to your car, they said. Make it look like you OD'd."

Slow Bear sat up. "But I did. I died."

"For, like, a few minutes, maybe."

"What?"

The girl held up a little tube between her fingers, with a little flared head on top. "Narcan. I had to use a couple to get you back. This doctor client sneaks them in to us. Saved some asses, I tell you."

He squinted, trying to take it all in.

"You've got to get out of here, though. Quickly. There's another door."

"It's guarded. They're all guarded."

"The guards are distracted."

He grabbed the armrest on the aisle and lifted himself off the floor. Wobbly. The girl stood, too, and she was very short. She had tossed her heels into one of the seats, and looked like a child going out to play barefooted. Except she had track marks down one of her arms.

"Why? What are you doing, helping me?"

"We've heard about you, looking for your girlfriend."

"She's not–"

"We've never seen someone try to save one of those girls. They all end up here before they get trucked out. Scared, can hardly speak English, or are just out of it. But once the sun goes down, they climb into the back of a van or a truck, and off they go."

"I lost her. She's off to Albuquerque, or wherever. She's gone."

She lifted her fingers to his lips, flicked off some dried vomit. "Then go find her. At least try. But get out of here. None of us want to watch you die again."

Slow Bear nodded, started for the exit. But he turned back to her. "Why are you here? Any of you? Is he keeping you all, like, prisoners?"

She gave him a shy smile, rubbed her hand up and down her arm. "No, not like that. We get free junk. That's what it's all about."

He peeked out the jet door, seeing what the girl meant by 'distraction,' as some of the guards were indulging in freebies, oblivious to the world beyond their cocks. He found the nearest exit. A guard still a little close, but considering the girl on her knees in front of him and his closed eyes, should be easy.

He skipped down the steps as light as he could, still not light enough. At least one guard looked up from having his head buried in tits to shout, "Hey!" before the girl pressed him back in there.

Slow Bear rushed to the exit nearest him, not even two feet from the guard getting the blowie. He turned the knob and a metallic squeal lit up the joint. Gave it a push, then a pull, and it felt as if the whole hanger was going to fall in on him. He grit his teeth, preparing for another beating.

The guard getting the blowie opened his eyes, turned his face towards Slow Bear and got a good look, then grinned and closed his eyes again. "Ain't worth it."

Slow Bear tried the knob again a few more times before the door pulled open and Slow Bear hung on for dear life. The sunlight blinded him. He wondered if he was still a bit dead. He fell onto his hand and knees on the tarmac outside as the door slammed shut behind him.

Too weak to run. Too weak to care, almost. He expected

any second now that the goons would get their nuts off and remember to come get him.

So he waited.

And waited.

And waited.

Caught his breath and pushed up onto his knees. Still no one after him.

One knee.

Then he was standing again. Looked at his palm. Scuzzed and almost black. Looked ahead of him. Flat, dry, and scorched. Waves of heat coming off the asphalt.

His next move? His next move.

If he could get the girls inside to…no.

If he could arm himself and go back to Santana's office and wait…no.

If he could hide in the back of Manfred's SUV, then pop up with a knife and…no.

Sigh.

He could call the cops.

It took him almost an hour to walk back to some sort of civilization, albeit not much—a convenience store. It had once been a Circle-K, because that was still painted on the front where the more recent paint was flaking off. FREEDOM STORE, it was supposedly called now. But the broken lit sign at the edge of the lot said it was a BP. Whatever.

Slow Bear thought about how he had been to the other side—actually dead—and come back only to be faced with this not-so-pearly gate.

Lo and behold, there was still an actual working payphone of the nineteen eighties variety. Luckily he still had some cash in his pocket—a crumpled ten and a five torn in three places.

The guy at the counter wouldn't give him change. He looked too old to be doing this job, too young to be retired. Nametag said 'Gil.'

Slow Bear picked up a pack of sugar-free gum and tossed it onto the counter.

"Five dollar minimum purchase."

"Bullshit. Show me."

"It's today only, just for one-armed Indians."

Motherfucker.

He went back into the aisles, picked up a king-sized Snickers and a bag of jerky. He hated jerky He put the Snickers and the gum back, though, because the jerky was mighty fucking expensive.

Now he was over the 'minimum.' He hand over the ten and told Gil, "All in change, please."

"You'll take what I give you. I'm rounding up."

Slow Bear slammed his palm flat on the counter. "Goddamn you, I need to use the phone!"

"That's not my problem."

"I've got three dollars and fourteen cents coming to me, and I want that in change, Gil. Or do you want me to wait for your manager and raise all sorts of hell?"

"I used to be an oilman, you know!" Gil gave it back just as loud. "I'm only doing this because the patch is drying up and I've got to send something home to my kids, if they're even mine, and their whore of a mother."

Slow Bear took a step back, staring. Waiting.

Then he said, "That's not my problem."

The counter man reached into the till, grabbed a handful of quarters, and threw them at Slow Bear. "Here, you want change? There's change! Now get the fuck out of my store before I use this hockey stick down below to whip your hide!"

The coins stung. There would be welts later. Slow Bear scrabbled as many quarters off the floor as he could while Gil was still leaning over the counter and yelling full bore.

Slow Bear ran to the phone and caught his breath. Looked in his hand. He'd gotten five quarters. A big net loss. Then he remembered that he didn't know what number to call for the cops, anyways. Except nine-one-one, that is, and nine-one-one was free.

Well ain't that all that? And no jerky to show for it either.

He walked over to the phone, picked up the receiver. It was

hot, of course, but also sticky, and Slow Bear did not want to think about why that might be. He wedged the receiver between his ear and shoulder and dialed.

The dispatcher, a pissy-sounding woman. "Nine-one-one. What's your emergency?"

"Hello, hi, yeah, is there a detective I can talk to?"

"Sir, this is nine-one-one, for emergencies only. Do you have an emergency?"

"Yeah, yeah, I do, I have an emergency, but really, is there someone I can talk to? It's not like a full-fledged response sort of emergency, but–"

"Sir."

"But more like–"

"Sir."

"Just transfer me to a detective, please? I don't know the number."

A huff from the dispatcher. "You really shouldn't call nine-one-one unless it's a current emergency. You could be hogging up the lines for a real one."

"Please, would you just…okay?"

A sniff and then a click. Another couple clicks. Slow Bear wondered if it was too late, if Santana had moved the girls and guards and all the rest while Slow Bear was walking here.

Then someone else picked up. A man with a drawl that belonged a thousand miles away from North Dakota. Probably another import–more oilmen meant more cops.

"Yeah-llo?"

"Listen, I don't have much time. But you guys, you'll need to hurry, and you need to keep it on the down low."

"Now settle, settle down now. How about we start with your name?"

"No, you don't need my name. Listen, there's a man. A well-known man, but still. His name is Santana. Now, if you go out to the airport at the edge of town, find this big-ass hangar, bigger than all the others, and look inside, you'll find human trafficking."

"Is that so?"

"It's a whorehouse. A special sort of whorehouse. It's the Mile High Club."

"Mile High? For real?"

"Yes sir." Maybe he could pull this off. "I'm a retired police officer myself, and Santana just tried to kill me out there. And my friend is missing. They kidnapped her and sent her away."

"Lordy."

"I know. She's on her way to some godforsaken place, a sex slave probably. But you guys, you can help us here. You can bust the place. If you can't get Santana, get his right-hand man Manfred. That's M-A-N Fred. Manfred. Find out where they sent my friend, and save those other ladies from whatever the fuck this all is."

Quiet from the other end. Well, not really. There was a sound like someone sucking his gums.

"Still there?"

The drawl returned. "So you're telling me there's a brothel hidden in plain sight at the airport—"

"Yes sir."

"And Mister Santana, who, you're right, is pretty well-known around these parts, is some sort of criminal mastermind—"

"Yes sir."

"And...and...and, you think that's all one big secret?"

"What?"

"You think I don't spend several nights a week out at the Mile High Club with my law enforcement brethren thanks to Mister Santana giving us a lifelong membership, no charge?"

Uh oh. Manfred had warned him: Because they work for us.

"Never mind."

"No, now you wait, son. You're the one-armed boy, aren't you? We've been on watch for you."

"It's been nice talking to you, forget I said anything."

"Where you calling, from a payphone? There are only three left in the whole city, so if you stay put, I can have some officers come pick you up—"

Slow Bear hung up. He started crying. Not loud or anything, but the waterworks started like a burst pipe. He moaned, "It's all my fault. She's gone, and it's all my fault, goddamnit, shit fuck!"

"Dude?"

He looked up to see Gil standing in the doorway, two-handing his hockey stick.

"Are you alright?"

Slow Bear nodded, wiped his eyes, and said, "Sure."

He was somehow able to keep himself hidden until later that evening. Wandering around behind stores, walking through trailer parks. He'd catch a glimpse of squad cars every now and then, prowling, but they never saw him. He even saw Manfred's SUV rolling slow not even a block away, but once again, he got lucky.

The only other thing he could think to do was go back to the car. Lady's car. She wouldn't be needing it anymore, and that gave Slow Bear a catch in his throat. He wondered if the cops or Santana's people might be staking it out, waiting for him to return. He'd have to be extra careful before trying to approach it, then.

There he was, outside Walmart as the sun started to sink and the sound of rattling grocery carts and screaming kids did his nerves a good one. The sign over the Sam's Choice vending machine said '0.00,' so he pressed a button and, lo and behold, a free cola dropped into the slot. Slow Bear took it, opened it, and took big gulps. He wished it was orange juice instead of this sugary goop but don't look a gift soda in the mouth, right? After all, he could've been dead instead.

Deep breath for courage.

He started for the back of the lot, looking this way and that, trying to find the watchers. Like, that couple sitting in that car…no, just smoking a little dope, he could smell it now. Or, there were a couple of trucks parked opposite, the drivers in conversation…no, just some good ol' boys. One sheriff's squad car…but it was empty.

The closer he got to the little shitty import, the more emboldened he felt, his stride lengthening as he kept on unmolested. Yeah. No one was going to lay a finger on him. Okay, so someone had stolen nearly all their shit through the broken window, but that was okay. He stepped around to the driver's door, dropped his ass into the bucket seat, and felt victorious.

Until he realized the reason he made it is because no one gave a shit.

Santana and Manfred and all the other goons who worked for him, all the corrupt cops and deputies, everyone else in this town who depended on the big man for a paycheck and then a way to spend it all, as far as they were concerned Slow Bear was nothing. A gnat not worth squashing. Unimportant. They'd already moved on. So they'd tried to kill him, failed, and oh well, hope he learned his lesson.

Thing was, as he tightened his grip on the steering wheel…he had.

He'd learned a good one.

Lady was gone in the worst way, it was all his fault, and the bad guys got away scot-free.

A quick look down at himself. Filthy with sweat-caked dust, a misbuttoned shirt with his own blood and sick all over it. Torn jeans, chafed balls, bloody knees. The odor like roadkill. He was lucky to be alive.

That's some fucking luck for you.

Slow Bear: alive and well. Lady: tortured, drugged…he didn't want to think what else.

How many women every day? How many? And how many people turned their heads? And how many men were swimming in the cesspool?

Jesus.

So…what now?

If he went home, he'd eventually have to explain himself to The Hat and Trevor. God only knew what they'd do to him. Prison? Worse?

He cranked up the car, pulled it out of the lot, and pointed it towards the rez.

When you've got nowhere left to go, might as well go home.

CHAPTER 16

Slow Bear slept humped over the steering wheel on the side of the road, fully expecting to be rousted by a state trooper and dragged away to jail, where at least he might get a good nap in. But no one bothered him through the long night, and once the first light of day stabbed at his eyes he pulled back onto the road home for sure, with an aching back added to his list of woes.

Prison wouldn't be so bad. Sure, he'd be locked up with a lot of guys he'd busted as a cop, but he was still respected by them. He'd given them breaks, even though he charged cash or favors. He'd allowed the machinery of crime to keep flowing across the rez and into the oil fields. He'd worked out the kinks when they arose. And finally, he'd gotten his arm blown the fuck off in the line of duty, which made it hard for the injured vets in jail to hold a grudge when he'd been hurt nearly as bad as they had.

At least, that's what he imagined. Could be Slow Bear was walking headfirst into his own brutal rapes, beatings, and eventual murder.

Criminals. They could be tricky.

The wind was dry and hot on his face. The needle was near empty, but Slow Bear was sure he could make it. What would he do with the car, though? Hand it over to Lady's parents? Let Trevor have it? Park it outside the trailer as a reminder?

Trying to figure it out hurt his brain. Let future Slow Bear deal, not this one. He needed a shower. He needed orange juice. He needed to mainline some heroin.

Like, why not? What did he have to strive for now besides

numbing himself, sitting up on his trailer, watching the stars? Fade away instead of burning out. Simple joys.

Something felt wrong as soon as he crossed the line onto the rez. All out of whack. Maybe it was all in his head. It was like the air smelled wrong. The quality of light was dimmed. The road sounded hollow. He was a man out of time. It was more likely he had changed rather than the rez. Everything was the same, just filtered through his busted senses. So onward he drove.

At the point Slow Bear should've seen his trailer in the distance, he did not.

Had to be a mistake. He was remembering wrong. Any mile now he'd watch it grow from the size of a peanut into his beautiful Richardson Bi-Level.

Another mile. Another mile. And another.

Now the surroundings were very familiar. He'd driven this road countless times. He knew the trees, what few there were. The two metal posts that used to hold up a pro-life ad. The eternal garbage pile, always slightly smoldering.

But no sign of his trailer.

It should be there. It has always been there. He'd moved it there himself and hooked it up and that's his home. What happened to his home?

Closer still, the lone tree in his yard right where he left it. His truck, held together by chewing gum, was still right there. His cheap gas barbecue grill, still there, still rusted, still hadn't been used since the third day after he bought it. But the trailer, not there.

He climbed out of the car, numb and angry all at once, a feeling he'd never felt before. A big blank spot where the Richardson Bi-Level trailer used to be. Well, except for the upside down plastic Adirondack chair, which must have fallen off the top when they took it. The power line and TV cable he'd rigged—stolen and stolen, of course—were swinging from their pole.

There were plenty of tire tracks, many of them starting to disappear as the dust blew around. Still, evidence that someone brought a big truck, hooked the trailer to the back end, and drove it right on down the road.

Hand on his hip. Not sure what to say, what to think. Not sure where he was going to sleep tonight. Maybe right here, in the car. He didn't even have enough money for his next meal.

So sad, so sad.

He heard the flapping before he saw the piece of paper stapled to the tree, one of the corners having already come undone, another held down by the handle of a borrowed shovel he'd forgotten to use. It hadn't been there before. He stepped over, ripped the rest off the bark and gave it a look.

A receipt from the rez police. They'd impounded the trailer. Exactly what Trevor had threatened to do. Slow Bear hadn't believed him. If he wanted it back, he would need to pay some fines, pay for some licenses, and pay to have the trailer moved to a proper trailer park instead of out here on land he didn't own.

Of course, he'd never own the trailer park land, either. He'd just pay stupidly high rent forever to a landlord who didn't give a shit about the upkeep of the park, while Slow Bear would end up surrounded by the very sort of people he'd moved out here to get away from.

No more nights on the roof, quietly watching the stars.

No more miles of nothing between him and that hit of H he craved and would easily get if it was everywhere.

No more.

He crumpled up the receipt. Couldn't afford the fines, the fees, the rent.

That left him one option then.

He climbed into his Nissan and started for town.

Slow Bear had cousins all over the rez. Not a surprise. For example, Trevor, the police chief. And there was probably some distant thread, taut to the point of snapping, between him and The Hat. But there were also the others, some he barely knew, some he'd grown up with, some he'd lost touch with.

Like the one he was going to see right now. Guy named Desi Lone Fight. They'd drank a lot together during their teenage years, gone to see concerts in Fargo—Slipknot, Marilyn Manson, Mastodon—pretended to start a band with two pawn shop guitars. Drifted apart eventually, after Slow Bear became a cop and Desi lost his license after too many DUIs, the last one killing a family of four.

He had eventually gotten paroled and turned into a hermit. But he still had a sweet Ford F-350 that was practically brand new except for the huge dents all across the front where it had ripped the dead family's Impala to shreds. All it did now was sit on the lawn, killing the grass beneath it, even though Desi kept it washed and the tires aired up despite him never being able to drive it again.

So Slow Bear would drive it instead. He pulled up at near one in the morning. The extra key was hidden behind the back license plate. He left his Nissan on the curb and climbed into Desi's behemoth Ford with its glacier white base and purple metal flake panthers on both sides.

Cranked that puppy up, let it roar, so Desi would know he was taking it. Then shifted into drive and spun his tires, ripping up the yard, as he shot off down the street.

Only a few minutes later, he was staring at the impound lot gate, a tall chain link loaded with signs like 'No Trespassing' and 'Keep Out' and 'Under Surveillance.'

Fuck that.

You know what? Slow Bear wanted them to know.

Pedal down. Straight for the gate.

Straight on through…

…to the other side.

The fence broke apart like tin foil and wrapped around the front end. The truck didn't even jolt except for the padlock and chain exploding into the windshield, giant crater cracking all around.

No sirens, no spotlights. Still, someone would notice. A sleepy security guard, or a rez cop who'd pulled the long straw. A part-timer wired on coffee in a room the size of a closet watching a camera feed.

Slow Bear slid to a stop in a dust cloud. He got out, tossed the fence off the front of the truck and looked around. Impounded cars the owners couldn't afford to get out of hock, probably because the fines cost more than the cars were worth anymore. Some jet skis on trailers, no idea why anyone would need those up here. Some oil trucks and equipment. And there, among a couple of RVs and a badly mauled single-wide, his Richardson Bi-Level in all its red-and-chrome glory.

It wasn't the simplest job even for a two-armed man, but Slow Bear was determined. He backed the Ford to the trailer, hitched it, chained it, didn't bother hooking up the brake lights. It had taken a little longer than expected, and still, no one had come to challenge him. In fact, he stood in front of the truck for a few minutes, catching his breath, waiting for the inevitable.

Well, didn't seem that was going to be tonight.

Slow Bear shook his head, climbed into the Ford, and pulled out of the lot. Time to go home.

The inside was completely trashed. Everything rattled, broken, smashed, and spilled. It was dark inside. It stank. Slow Bear turned in circles with his hand on his hip. His guns had been taken. But he checked his hiding spot deep in the springs of his couch and found his sawed-off twelve-gauge and back-up .357, only four bullets in it. He checked under his mattress in the bedroom, where he'd cut out a space for an AK-47 and a bulletproof vest. Still there.

Fucking idiots.

He took all that to the sunroof, then came down, outside. He tossed his Adirondack chair up there, too.

Not going to bother unhooking the trailer from the truck.

Not going to bother with the electricity.

Here he was, home again. His trailer, his tree, his barbecue grill, Desi's truck and Lady's car.

The next step was to get ready for what was coming for him.

And if that turned out to be nothing at all, so much the better.

CHAPTER 17

It took until sunrise for the sirens to first echo in Slow Bear's
direction. He was long ready by then.

Sitting on the sundeck in his Adirondack chair. Jeans and
the vest, that was all he wore and nothing else. Barefoot. AK-
47 propped on his thigh, the other guns within reach. A big
glass of warm orange juice snugged in his lap. Sunglasses.

The sirens grew louder, the sheer insanity of them whistling
and crying across the prairie. It made Slow Bear smile. The
funnel of dust rising way off yonder looked like a twister.

He didn't move.

The early morning hours melted off and he had finally
climbed aboard the trailer and caught a glimpse of planets,
Jupiter and Venus shining bright as the black of night turned
midnight blue. But now all was gray and cold.

The closer the sirens, the closer the twister, the pinker the
light. When the full fury of the assault revealed itself, the
maddening noise, Slow Bear grooved on it like it was Pantera.

Nearly every vehicle in the rez police fleet, mostly trucks
and SUVs but also cop cars, with nearly every officer, both
full-time and reserve, packed into each one.

They were all coming for him.

At first, it was a line like a long boa constrictor. Then each
vehicle broke off and ran circles around the trailer before
taking their positions, all the cops leaping out together and
aiming any and all types of firearms at Slow Bear, who didn't
move a muscle.

One car in particular sat right in front of Slow Bear, no one
out and aiming yet. He knew this car. It was Trevor's personal
squad car. The man had a driver and everything. After a few
more minutes, Trevor slowly climbed from the passenger seat

holding a bullhorn, keeping the door open, but it would be a pretty lousy shield from this angle.

Trevor lifted the bullhorn to his mouth. "What the goddamned hell are you doing, Micah?"

"I failed, Trevor! I fucked it all up."

"Come down and tell me about it."

"I don't think so. I think you should all leave now, you filthy home thieves. Apologize and leave me alone."

"Okay, okay, I'm sure we can do that, if you'll come down."

Slow Bear stood from his chair, the AK dangling in his hand. The glass of orange juice tumbled and spilled at his feet. That got a chorus of "Don't fucking move!" from all the assembled cops.

Trevor bullhorned, "Take it easy, goddamn it! DO. NOT. SHOOT."

The cops stayed put.

Slow Bear, laughing and shaking now, "I fucked it all up, I said! What you told me to do, I fucked it up. I lost Lady. You should never have sent her with me! Look at what happened! Look at what I did!"

"Where is the girl? Is she inside?"

"I told you, I lost her! Kylie is gone, man. Gone."

Trevor pulled the bullhorn away and looked sick. The weight of it, him sending the girl with Slow Bear and her not coming back. He'd be bathing in a shit shower soon enough. Look at him. Pathetic. He turned and asked his driver for the radio handset. He spoke into it, listened, then spoke again. Then lifted the bullhorn.

"Come down here and we can deal with it."

Slow Bear shook his head. "I want The Hat!"

"What?"

"I want to see The Hat. I want him to come up here and talk to me."

"That's not going to happen."

"Tell him I want to see him! Fucking tell him!"

"Never gonna happen, Micah. But if you come on down, he'll meet you at the jail. We'll get you a lawyer there.

Everything by the book."

"Get me The Hat, man. Get him up here. Just me and him. Or," Slow Bear dropped the AK, grabbed the sawed-off, and held it tight under his chin. "Or I'll end this myself. Is that what you want? This whole story, I promise you, it'll come out. From the beginning to the end, I swear."

"You're not going to do it."

"Get me The Hat. I'm done with you."

Slow Bear plopped back down into the chair, sawed-off still under his chin, and ignored everything else Trevor had to say, everything his little minions shouted from around the trailer. Flat out pretended they didn't exist. Started humming Judas Priest songs. One-handed air guitar.

What were they going to do? Shoot him? Seriously?

What would he have done in the same situation in his cop days?

Oh, he would've shot the bastard. Absolutely.

Which is why he was a terrible cop.

It took nearly three more hours of siege for Trevor to finally bullhorn up, "Okay, The Hat's coming. He'll be here soon."

"Cool." Slow Bear stood, kept the gun pressed tight. "I've got to go inside and take a piss."

He was back in place on the sundeck when he saw another twister in the distance, growing larger until The Hat's sleek black Lincoln Navigator came into view, hauling ass. The Hat was nothing if not full bore. Slow Bear hoped he'd interrupted the man taking a shit or eating a steak, something like that.

The Hat drove himself. He pulled right through the barrier of squad cars until he was front and center. He climbed out without a look up at Slow Bear and stomped over to Trevor's side. He wore his barn coat, jeans, most worn-in boots, a trucker cap instead of his big-ass hat, aviator shades over a frown and a goatee. A thin, frayed braid of hair trailed down his back. He was a plump man, but plump like a weightlifter. Even at his advanced age, he could still knock anyone's block

118

off.

Slow Bear watched and waited.

After Trevor filled him in on the details, The Hat turned to Slow Bear and, without a bullhorn, said, "You've lost all your marbles, son."

"I never had any marbles, sir."

"Get your ass down here so I can give it a proper kicking."

Slow Bear shook his head. "How about you come up here, have a talk?"

"You're in no position to make demands."

"Come up and sit awhile. I'll let you have my chair."

The Hat turned to Trevor. "Any reason you ain't shot him yet?"

"Sir…" Trevor shrugged.

"You really need that thing?" He pointed to the bullhorn. "The boy is right there."

Trevor fiddled with the bullhorn a little before The Hat slapped it out of his hands.

"All right, I'm coming up."

He started for the trailer door, but Trevor grabbed him by the arm. The Hat shook him off. "He's not going to kill me, asshole. Grow up."

The Hat tromped his bulk to the trailer door, then loudly up the steps to the sundeck. As he'd promised, Slow Bear rose from his chair and offered it to The Hat.

The big man sat down. The roof creaked.

"I'm here now, and this had better be good. You're already fucked from way down low to way up high."

"I'm sorry, sir."

"Sorry for what? For killing that man? Sorry isn't a get out of jail free card, so you might as well own it. Vlad was stupid as oil is black. Put the notch on your gun and carry that with you."

"I will, sir. But that's not how I failed."

Big sigh. The Hat took off his sunglasses. The eyes behind were small, surrounded by bloat, and very tired. "Sit down. And put that fucking gun away."

Slow Bear sat cross-legged and lowered the gun to his lap. Felt like a little kid listening to his teacher tell a story.

"What happened over there?"

"I lost my friend. Kylie. They took her, Santana and his goons. Took her right out from under me. I didn't know it was them until it was too late." His face went red. The tears rolling down boiled away. "I mean, I sold you out, sir. I told him why I was there so I could come back home. But then I lost her…"

"Did you check the fridge?"

"What?"

The Hat waved that off. "Never mind. Goddamnit, son, I'm sorry to hear that. A goddamn shame, what's happening to those girls. Our girls. Any girls."

"He roped me in. Told me he'd help me find her if I worked for him. But it was all a lie. It was him all along."

"I'll be damned."

"Did you know? Did you already know he was into that?"

"No, I can't say I did. Rumors, of course, but so many to choose from. I'm sorry."

"I've got nothing else to keep me going. I lost my friend, and she's long gone. Trevor stole my home, I stole it back. And here we are."

The Hat rubbed his tiny eyes with thumb and a finger. "Yep. Here we are."

Neither of them spoke for a while. Slow Bear stared at the whirling lights on the squad cars below. The Hat sniffed. A glance down at Trevor showed him with arms crossed, leaning against the front of his car.

"Well." The Hat lifted himself from the Adirondack chair and stepped aside. "What's it going to be? Suicide? Suicide by cop? Prison? Tell me what you want."

"I don't want any of that. I want you to leave me alone."

"It's too late. Look at it down there, all because of you. If I want this reservation to keep the status quo, I can't let you go around willy nilly, stealing and destroying, killing. No, son, I just can't."

"Okay. I understand."

"So what's it going to be? Come down with me, we'll do the best we can for you. I'll make sure you get a fair shake."

Seriously, what else had Slow Bear been doing all this time since he lost his arm? A prison of his own design, right? But at least in that prison he had the trailer, the sundeck at night, the whole cosmos, and, before, a few precious hours with Lady each day. Without any of that, what was life going to be like?

No fresh-squeezed orange juice, that was for sure.

He was ready for the next step. The inevitable.

"Sir, I respectfully decline. I think I'll stay up here."

The whirling lights on the cop cars. The hot wind on his back.

"You sure about that?"

"Pretty sure."

"And you know how this is going to end?"

A long beat, then. "Better than you."

Down below, he picked out the people he used to work with. Some he'd known all his life, some since high school, some whose relatives he knew, some he'd never met.

He lifted the sawed off shotgun to his chin again.

"All right. Goodbye, son, you stupid motherfucker."

The Hat lumbered back down the stairs, out to Trevor, spoke to him a handful of minutes, then got in his SUV, drove away as fast as he'd come.

Trevor picked up the bullhorn from the ground, dusted it off, and held it to his lips. "All right. Ball's in your court."

Okay, Slow Bear thought. That's where it'll stay.

He held them off until sundown. More police cars showed up, this time from the Sheriff's Department. Maybe just looky-loos. Then an ambulance showed up. That was thoughtful of them. Then the van from the funeral home.

Oh my.

Trevor had kept quiet, somehow managed to hold onto his cool. Same as all the other cops. Not one single shot fired. Not in anger, nor in boredom. They all stood their ground, waiting for that next swat of the ball.

And Slow Bear sat on his sundeck the whole time, not moving. The sun enflamed his skin, sweat pouring from all over. He licked salty, cracked lips, desperate for water, but not giving Trevor the satisfaction.

Then the sky blazed orange, red, pink, then purple, more shadows than light, and that was when Slow Bear rose as if from the dead. Double-vision. Hallucinating his ancestors. Not those in feathers and bison skins, but his grandfathers–bastard crusty men who never told Slow Bear they loved him, but would take him fishing and hunting. Both had chain-smoked and died relatively young–fifty-seven and sixty-one. They hated each other. They were just alike.

Both helped Slow Bear rise to his feet and stagger on pins-and-needles legs until he fell. They walked beside him as he crawled to the steps and tumbled down into his trailer.

His mother's dad said, "Better than a heart attack, I reckon."

His father's dad said, "Shut up, clown."

Slow Bear laughed. Man, those two could hold some grudges. He stood, held the wall while the blood returned to his legs. He made it to the bed. Underneath, he had hidden a gallon jug of gasoline he'd siphoned from Desi's truck.

Time to end this.

Trevor banged on the door. "Micah? Micah? I'm going to come in there! I swear! Micah!"

Didn't matter. Pretty soon, Trevor wouldn't want to be anywhere near the joint.

By the time Slow Bear reappeared on the sunroof, flinging the last of the gasoline here and there, even on his Adirondack chair, the smoke was already billowing from the trailer. The windows popped and let out more smoke, more flames. The plastic burned into slick, oily tendrils, twisting into the air. The smell, burning rubber and fur. Crispy and toxic.

The gallon jug in Slow Bear's hand caught on fire, and he slung it out into the crowd as if he was a rock god at a concert.

The cops shot at it, finally a target for them. Slow Bear raised his arm above his head. Mickey in Fantasia. The flames trickled higher, the smoke darker. Trevor fought with the locked door below, shouting Micah's name, burning his fingers. Other cops began shooting through the fire obscuring Slow Bear.

But the same way they couldn't see him, he couldn't see them. He trusted the laws of physics and biology. He hoped the fire was a blinding spectacle in the near-night, fucking with everyone's eyes.

And when he couldn't take the heat coming up from below, scorching his bare feet, and the fire threatening to overwhelm him, Slow Bear ran.

And he jumped.

And…that's when the magic happened.

CHAPTER 18

They had no running water. All they had were small fire extinguishers in the trucks of each squad car, and those did nothing to stop the inferno that soon spread to the Ford pickup truck, and then to the lone tree, even to the handle of the borrowed shovel and the once-used barbecue grill.

The army of cops and their cars had to back off for their own safety, watching Hell unfold before them.

By the time a fire tanker arrived, there wasn't much trailer or truck left. The volunteer firemen did what they could with what they had, which was to turn everything to a sopping pit of mud and soot.

The remaining officers then had to search that pit for the remains of Slow Bear.

Almost all of them had watched him jump. None of them could agree where he landed.

Or even if he landed.

As if he had been swept away by the Creator, his four souls scattered to the heavens and the earth.

But Trevor told them, "Find his bones."

They waited for morning. With the sunrise came even more ugliness. Police caked in sludge, the stench of men relieving themselves into the dirt, the gagging sounds from breathing chemical odors all through the night. Men, strong men, passing out from the stress of it.

But nowhere was found one bone of Micah "Slow Bear" Cross.

Trevor grilled each and every one of his officers, the firemen, and the deputies who'd come by to gawk. None of them could agree to what they saw once Slow Bear had leapt from the sundeck of the Richardson Bi-Level. Some said he caught fire. Some said he landed, rolled, and started running across the plain. Still others said they shot him on the way down, and he should be here.

But…he wasn't.

He just wasn't.

He was gone.

Trevor called it by late afternoon. They would need to send forensics people out to get a better idea of what happened. All they'd done so far was contaminate the crime scene–the trailer pit, the frame of the F-350 pick-up, the roasted tree, and, surprisingly, a shitty little import, name badge fallen off years before, that had somehow survived the flames.

Trevor told his best men to search that car, high and low, inside and out, even tear it apart if they had to. He watched them go over it, wincing, knowing it was Kylie's car. The poking, the prodding, the removal of the dash board, the seats, all of her things in the back thrown out onto the ground, felt like a further violation. He hoped Slow Bear's story was not true, that she really hadn't been snatched by sex traffickers, but…how could he ever know for sure?

When his squad was done, they'd found nothing but a lot of hot beer in the trunk. Nothing else suspicious.

Trevor dismissed them. Before long, he had a guy tape off the whole plot, then told everyone to go home.

He pronounced Slow Bear missing. That was as far as he'd go.

The platoon of squad cars, the fire tanker, the ambulance, and the van all left a lot slower than when they showed up. The dust settled and the world reset to the quiet emptiness that Slow Bear had loved so much.

Not one of the cops who'd searched Lady's car had noticed the depression in the dirt beneath, and the bundle of drinking straws poking out from the surface.

When Slow Bear finally felt it was safe, he lifted his head, which was covered by a cardboard box he'd fucked with to keep the dirt out. Then he'd poked another hole in the side for the bundle of straws so he could breathe. The rest of the prairie dirt covering him fell away, and Slow Bear rolled from under the car. He stayed flat on his back, gulping in the gnarly-smelling air, still good enough for him. He stretched his limbs, his back, and his neck. Hours and hours, lying still, in the shallow hole he'd spent more hours and hours digging the night before with the borrowed shovel. He'd forgotten who he borrowed it from, but all that was left was the blade. Listening for voices, feeling for vibrations, hoping he'd done enough to not get caught.

It had worked. He'd lost the Richardson Bi-Level, but face it, he'd already lost that the moment the police towed it.

There was nothing left for him on the rez.

That was when he had decided, absolutely. Kylie was still out there in America somewhere, being tortured in God only knew what ways, and Slow Bear had run away. He'd come home with his tail between his legs.

Bullshit. This time, he was determined to find her or die trying.

The gallon of gas he'd siphoned from Desi's truck was not the only gallon he'd sucked out of the tank. The rest, he put into this shitty little import. It had many more miles to carry him.

He'd stashed a change of clothes in his cardboard box, so he changed into a t-shirt, track shorts, and flip-flops. He looked at Lady's belongings, strewn across the ground, along with the plastic from the dash and the passenger seat, back bench seat. He didn't need any of that. Shame about his guns, though, but he was sure he'd find more. He always did.

He took a last look around. Still a few crackles here and there. The barest film of smoke rising from the slop. He wondered how long it would take for nature to take control, make this place look like it had when he first moved the Richardson Bi-Level out here. He wondered if another tree would grow on this spot.

He turned to the West. To tomorrow. To Kylie.
I'm coming for you. I'm coming.

THE END

Also from Anthony Neil Smith and published by Fahrenheit Press

The Butcher's Prayer – Published October 2021

About the author

Anthony Neil Smith is the author of numerous crime novels, including the Billy Lafitte series (including YELLOW MEDICINE and HOGDOGGIN'), award-winning ALL THE YOUNG WARRIORS, plus CASTLE DANGER: WOMAN ON ICE, WORM, THE CYCLIST, and more.

He is an English Professor at Southwest Minnesota State University.

He likes cheap red wine and Mexcian food.

His dog is named Herman, and he is a good boy.

More books from Fahrenheit Press

Know Me From Smoke by Matt Phillips

Stella Radney, longtime lounge singer, still has a bullet lodged in her hip from the night when a rain of gunfire killed her husband. That was twenty years ago and it's a surprise when the unsolved murder is reopened after the district attorney discovers new evidence.

Royal Atkins is a convicted killer who just got out of prison on a legal technicality. At first, he's thinking he'll play it straight. Doesn't take long before that plan turns to smoke— was it ever really an option?

When Stella and Royal meet one night, they're drawn to each other. But Royal has a secret. How long before Stella discovers that the man she's falling for isn't who he seems?

"A beautifully written, brutal & brilliant slice of hardboiled crime fiction. A Knockout."

Pure by Jo Perry

Caught in a pincer movement between the sudden death of Evelyn (her favourite aunt) and the Corona virus, Ascher Lieb finds herself unexpectedly locked down in her aunt's retirement community with only Evelyn's grief-stricken dog Freddie for company.

As the world tumbles down into a pandemic shaped rabbit-hole Ascher is wracked with guilt that her aunt was buried without the Jewish burial rights of purification. In order to atone for this dereliction of familial duty, Ascher – in her own words 'a profane, unobservant, atheist Jew, frequent liar and grieving loser' –volunteers to become the newest member of Valley Haverim Chevra Kadisha, a Jewish burial society on-call twenty-four-seven during lockdown and performing Mitzvot at no cost to the bereaved.

What follows is a journey through the insanity of lockdown in Los Angeles as Ascher attempts to bring peace to a troubled soul, and perhaps in the end redemption for herself.

"The mystery will get under your skin, for sure, but the humanity of this novel will resonate far beyond the page."

Turbulence by Paul Gadsby

Accidentally shooting a civilian during a bungled heist was bad enough, but when they upset the local criminal kingpin as a result of their ineptitude, newbie bank-robbers Birty & Cole figured the best thing to do was split town, and fast.

Smart plan - at least it was till everything went south, again.

An armed robbery is an unusual event which affects the lives of everyone touched by it and in this tour de force Paul Gadsby traces the lines of influence and connection that run through the lives of the people unwittingly caught up in Birty & Cole's heist.

The story is woven through the lives and perspectives of many characters - everyone from the bank staff and customers who witnessed the raid, to the journalists covering the case.

This remarkable novel from Brit-Noir legend Paul Gadsby ignores the usual crime fiction tropes of 'robbers on the run' and instead becomes a vivid study into cause & effect that will keep you gripped until the very last ripple fades away.

"Gadsby has really come into his own with this book - the writing & the storytelling are simply superb."

Made in the USA
Coppell, TX
11 June 2022

78720038R00080